I WANTED YOU TO SEE WHAT I
CAN DO SO YOU WILL BELIEVE
WHAT I SAY, MISS BRIGHT EYES.
YOU KNOW WHAT YOU HAVE TO
DO. DO IT OR YOUR FACE IS
NEXT.

"So Marshall and I are in bed, Mr. Denson,
a little high off some southern Oregon bud
Marshall bought for us last week. We're watching reruns of *Saturday Night Live* and eating
some Titanic Taco nachos Marshall brought
with him. He'd been bringing me big boxes of
frozen burritos and stuff."

"And along comes a guy with a ski mask
over his face?"

"Along comes the guy with ski mask. Two
holes for his eyes, one for his mouth, that's
it. The guy's so quick I don't get a good look
at him." Melinda looked like she was about
ready to cry.

Willie said, "The guy beats the hell out of
Marshall and gives Melinda the note."

Tor Books by Richard Hoyt

FISH STORY

RICHARD HOYT

TOR

A TOM DOHERTY ASSOCIATES BOOK

FISH STORY

Copyright © 1985 by Richard Hoyt

Reprinted by arrangement with Viking Penguin Inc.

First Tor printing: August 1987

A TOR Book

Published by Tom Doherty Associates, Inc.
49 West 24 Street
New York, N.Y. 10010

ISBN: 0-812-50491-7
CAN. ED.: 0-812-50492-5

Library of Congress Catalog Card Number: 83-40644

Printed in the United States of America

0 9 8 7 6 5 4 3 2 1

for Janice Johnson

The skies they were ashen and sober;
　　The leaves they were crisped and sere—
　　The leaves they were withering and sere;
It was night in the lonesome October
　　Of my most immemorial year.

—EDGAR ALLAN POE, from *Ulalume*

1 MELINDA

The late summer salmon harvest had been poor for yet another year in the Pacific Northwest, but it was in and counted before the fish story began. Willie Prettybird and I were facing dislocation from our old darts haunt at the Pig's Alley, which wasn't the best start. The Pig's view of Puget Sound was too good and the colorful hubbub of Pike Place Market was too handy for Tontos like Willie and Lone Rangers like me. Willie and I knew that and weren't surprised when the Pig's Alley was sold, scheduled for replacement by a restaurant to be called Le Cuisine de Pacifique.

Willie went into a fruitcake imitation when we heard the news. "Oh, Jesus, Denson," he lisped. His wrists drooped like wet towels. Willie was a Native American, a real Indian—not a make-believe or a pretend one. "It's just so wonderful!" he said. "All those sweet, sweet people will be coming down here to eat food from Paris, France."

I said, "There'll be waiters dressed like butlers in old movies."

"There'll be cute little tables with candles in the center. The talk'll be as soft as the wings of a dove." Willie fluttered his fingers and grinned. He made kissing sounds with his lips. Kiss. Kiss. Kiss.

"The menfolk'll wear blue blazers with nifty little buttons," I said. I held my wrists up and admired imaginary blue blazer cuffs.

"Oh, yes, and the ladies'll take extra time with their makeup, maybe wear a dress to show a little boob there." Willie Prettybird cupped his hands on his chest by way of demonstration. "They'll know the food is good because there won't be much of it and the prices'll be outrageous. The gentleman will be casual when he pulls his VISA—no swallowing or grinding of teeth. And the message to m'lady? If you please, Mr. Denson."

"This guy's got bucks. Lean forward," I said. I pretended to leer at Willie's make-believe breasts. That's the way it was with Willie and me, Chingachgook and Natty Bumppo, Chief Dumbshit and the Natural Assholete.

Melinda Prettybird came to me for help on the next to the last night at the Pig's Alley. The final, melancholy hours were upon us. The drinkers and talkers at the Pig's faced the end with spirit—agitated, euphoric with nostalgia, they decided to start a memorable wake a day before the death was official. Under the circumstances and considering the victim, they said, that was the correct thing to do. It was a Friday night, and when the jazz band arrived the drinking would begin in earnest. The regulars would close the Pig's out on Friday and Saturday nights. On Sunday they would rest.

Willie Prettybird and I played 301 late Friday afternoon, waiting for the wake to begin in earnest. I was sitting on a double-ten to beat Willie Prettybird when I spotted her walking through the crowd, coming right at us. She was an Indian with a walk that turned heads. I'd never seen Melinda but I suspected it might be her. I looked at Willie.

Willie laughed. "My sister. I told her to meet us here." Willie was pleased at my reaction. He was proud of Melinda. "She's a looker, didn't I tell you?"

"Well, setting up an old pardner, eh? Your sister'll be in good hands with me, Willie, you know that."

Ordinarily that would have earned a put-down, but Willie was suddenly serious. "We've got a little problem we need to talk to you about, Denson." He rose to greet his sister.

"Is this your friend John Denson?" Melinda Prettybird was a short, extraordinarily pretty woman dressed in blue jeans and a checkered shirt. She had large, flirtatious brown eyes. Her glistening black hair was done in a handsome braid and fell to the small of her back.

I rose to shake her small hand.

"I'm pleased to meet you, Mr. Denson." Melinda gave me a smile that was both shy and provocative. Melinda Prettybird was Indian-beautiful, which is to say exotic and Asian, not

white-woman-beautiful. She looked me straight
on with those flirtatious brown eyes. They were
enough to make a man's knees buckle.

Willie and I ordinarily talked about out-darts
and the Sonics. We razzed and were razzed in
turn. We didn't talk a whole lot about family
although I knew his sister, Melinda, had had
her ups and downs. After Melinda had taken a
seat, Willie got right on with it. "A man in a
ski mask beat up one of Melinda's boyfriends
last night, put him in a hospital." He cleared
his throat. "Crashed right into the bedroom."

Melinda looked embarrassed. "Last night was
the third time," she said.

I looked at Willie. "Bedroom attacks? What
are you talking about?"

"The guy says Melinda's next." Willie was
one worried Redskin. "It's her ex-husband,
Mike Stark. We're sure of it. Listen to this,
Denson. Tell him, Melinda."

"I knew there was something wrong with
Mike from the beginning, Mr. Denson." Melinda's eyes were disappointed, bitter. "Big-deal
history professor. Big-deal fishing rights expert.
Why would a guy like that marry a Cowlitz
squaw eighteen years younger than himself? In
three years of marriage he never got off my
case, not once. Claimed I was going to bed
with every male in the city of Seattle. I couldn't
talk to a grocery clerk without him freaking
out . . ."

Willie said, "A guy like that's not right
upstairs. You know that, Denson."

".... we had two sons before I packed my suitcases." Melinda fell silent. It was hard for her to continue.

I knew most of the story. The courts awarded Melinda nearly two hundred thousand dollars of Mike Stark's family money, which she promptly turned over to her brothers to help start a fishing business. Willie had gotten his start working part-time at the counter of a fish stall in the Pike Place Market and wound up managing the place. His brother, Rodney, worked as a deck hand on a commercial fishing boat. With a little help from the Small Business Administration, they launched the Prettybird Fish Company—with Rodney in charge of their four gillnet boats operating out of Astoria, Oregon, just off the mouth of the Columbia River.

There is no adequate way of saying how much Willie Prettybird appreciated his sister. Anybody who hurt Melinda hurt Willie. Younger brother, Rodney, felt the same way, only Rodney, under the influence of Old Granddad, was notorious for his temper.

"This was the third time? Why didn't you say something earlier, Willie?" I was irritated and let it show. I was Willie's friend, a private investigator. He should have come to me earlier.

"I didn't want him to," Melinda said. "I was embarrassed. The guy didn't say anything the first couple of times. I figured he'd give up. Last night was different."

"What happened last night?"

"I guess last night he let me know how crazy he really is."

"What's that?"

"He gave me this." Melinda opened her handbag and retrieved a note, which she unfolded on the table for me to read. The note, in large, handwritten block letters, said:

I WANTED YOU TO SEE WHAT I CAN DO SO YOU WILL BELIEVE WHAT I SAY, MISS BRIGHT EYES. YOU KNOW WHAT YOU HAVE TO DO. DO IT OR YOUR FACE IS NEXT.

Willie said, "Why did he give her a note, Denson? Why didn't he just threaten her?"

"I guess because he thought she might recognize his voice."

Willie was pissed. "Mike Stark."

I said, "Can you give me the details leading up to last night, Melinda? Everything you can think of."

"Tell him everything, sis. I'll kick his ass if he doesn't keep your confidence."

Melinda Prettybird sighed. "Well, I met a man named Marshall Collins, lives down in Tacoma. He's a nice guy. Things were going okay between us. He was real pleasant. He even liked the way I cook eggs." Melinda laughed at that. "I break the darn yolks every time. He even likes Michael and Bert—those are my little boys. Marshall runs one of those franchised taco places in Tacoma, the Titanic Taco." She stopped momentarily.

Willie said, "Tell him everything, sis. He'll need to know everything."

"I know, Willie, but it's hard."

"Denson's heard it all, I'm sure," he said.

"So Marshall and I are in bed, Mr. Denson, a little high off some southern Oregon bud Marshall bought for us last week. We're watching reruns of *Saturday Night Live* and eating some Titanic Taco nachos Marshall brought with him. He'd been bringing me big boxes of frozen burritos and stuff."

"And along comes a guy with a ski mask over his face?"

"Along comes the guy with ski mask. Two holes for his eyes, one for his mouth, that's it. The guy's so quick I don't get a good look at him." Melinda looked like she was about ready to cry.

Willie said, "The guy beats hell out of Marshall and gives Melinda the note."

"I think I better go to the ladies' room," Melinda said. She started to get up. She was fighting tears. "Listen, this is hard, you know. I've got Prib Ostrow sitting Michael and Bert. It isn't fair to take advantage of his good nature like this. What do you say you two play a few games of darts and come on down to my place. Give me a couple of hours and we can finish then. I'll be okay with Prib."

"Oh, sure, sis," Willie said. "I'll give you a call after a while. When you're ready, we'll come on over."

"Thank you, Willie. I appreciate all this, Mr. Denson."

"No problem," I said. A man would do almost anything for a woman with eyes like Melinda Prettybird's. I watched her small, vulnerable figure as Willie escorted her to her car.

The Pig's Alley regulars would have to do without us at the start of the wake.

2 RODNEY'S VOW

When Willie Prettybird returned to the Pig's, I let him know I was sore. He had it coming. "Listen, Chief Bungwad, why in the hell didn't you come to me earlier? I'm disease-free. I feed parking meters. It's dangerous and stupid to let something like that ride."

Willie ordered another pitcher of beer. We had some serious talking to do. "Your fee is what's wrong with you, Denson. This kind of thing is how you earn your living."

"What?" I couldn't believe he'd said that.

"What money we haven't spent on Rodney's boats and fixing nets, we've blown on the Cowlitz lawsuit, and that's the truth."

I said, "Willie, if I were a dentist and Melinda had a toothache, I wouldn't charge her for pulling the damned thing. If I were a doctor and you had hemorrhoids, I wouldn't charge for operating on your ass. We're talking about your sister, man."

"I always pay my way," Willie said.

"You always pay your own way," I mimicked his voice. "Okay, Chief, if you insist. Full tariff

9

it is. You have to be my doubles partner in the
Seattle Dart Classic. I don't mind being carried
by someone who can hit an out-dart. All I want
is glory and a trophy."

Willie looked like I'd socked him with a bill
for ten grand. "Man, you don't come cheap."

"You're the one who said you wanted to pay
your own way. Pride costs sometimes. You also
have to spring for my screw-top and raw
vegetables while I'm on the case. That could
add up."

"Just how much money you think a guy
makes selling fish, anyway?"

"Tut, tut, Willie. Let's not be cheap. I won't
have it. You get what you pay for. You're lucky
I don't drink corked wine." I took a sip of beer.
"Heap big warpath. Let's do it."

Willie leaned forward. "Okay, Kemosabe, only
I get to help. I can do legwork."

"Only if you tell me what Kemosabe means?"

"It means chickenshit," Willie said.

"Well, I resemble that," I said. "Now then,
are you telling me that Melinda didn't tell
Marshall about the first two beatings? The guy
just walks right in? She hasn't changed the
lock or anything?"

"Who'd have thought it would have happened a third time? It's been, what, six weeks
since the first time."

Whoa! Melinda Prettybird had an active social life. "And the lock?" I asked. "Did you
change the lock?"

"That's the crazy part. She's changed the

lock twice and he just walks right through. Tomorrow night I'm going over there and put some real locks on her door, maybe a couple of big old dead bolts."

"How bad was Marshall hurt?"

"Broken jaw, a few loose teeth, eyes swollen shut. Shit, John, you should've seen him—his face looks like a plate of refried beans."

The memory of Melinda's lovely brown eyes lingered with me. "The men around here would be a little better off if your sister weren't so good-looking, Willie. What did the cops say? You did call the cops, I assume."

"Sure, sure, we called the cops."

"What happened?"

"They went through a routine each time, you know. Both times they came back and said Mike Stark had an alibi. They said they don't have any idea who else it might be. They said they're doing their best. I always liked Mike Stark, Denson, you know that, but some guys bonk out when it comes to women. You just never know. When he and Melinda split, Mike said no other man would ever have her. No man. It all fits. He comes to pick up his kids; he knows who's seeing his ex."

"Cops take things one step at a time," I said.

"Just because Mike got along with Rodney and me doesn't mean Jack. He's an okay guy but an asshole to Melinda. Melinda's got some stories that'd make you shake your head. Hey, this's all a matter of court record."

I read the note again. "I suppose it's possible to interpret this a couple of ways."

Willie looked at the note himself. "Like how?"

"Judging from the papers every day there're a few salmon fishermen who don't exactly love you."

"Oh, come on," Willie said. "No reason for those guys to write little notes. It's Mike Stark. It has to be. He doesn't like the idea of Melinda's having a boyfriend."

"Did the cops tell you what they did?"

"Aw, come on, John. Do the cops do anything? I'm beginning to wonder if they give a shit. So what if a squaw's boyfriends get roughed up a little. You know how those things go."

I always thought Seattle cops were as honest as those in any large city. There were both winners and losers on the force, but it was hard to think Melinda had been treated casually because she was a Cowlitz. "I can't believe they're not trying," I said.

"The only thing wrong with my theory is Rodney says the guy isn't Mike. He says it's somebody else. He knows who it is."

"Ahh, brother Rodney knows who it is. Then there's good news."

Willie sat back and sighed. "Bad, bad, bad news. Rodney says he's gonna kill the son of a bitch."

I leaned forward. "Who? Who is he going to kill?"

"He won't say. That's all I know."

"Maybe it's Doug Egan," I said. "You're always talking about Egan's stunts. From what you've been saying, Rodney's lucky he hasn't drowned out there. Maybe Egan's upped the stakes. A little pressure on Melinda to get the Prettybird Fish Company out of their water."

"It's Mike Stark," Willie said.

I knew a little about Willie's fishing-rights lawsuit because he had gone over and over the logic of the Cowlitz case in our dart games. In the early 1850s, Governor Isaac Stevens signed various treaties to take care of the salmon fishing issue. The tribes in the center of the coast and in the north were taken care of first. In February 1855 Stevens met in council with the fish-eating tribes of the southwestern part of the state. The tribes didn't have governments and chiefs in the usual sense, so Stevens, needing someone to sign his treaty, drew up documents appointing various tribal elders as chiefs. The Governor said he would be back the next day to collect the signed treaty. The Indians then set about to celebrate their good fortune of a guaranteed one-half of the salmon entering their fishing grounds.

Alas, in the excitement an elder named Tleyuk, inspired by the paper appointing him Chief of the Chehalis, said the treaty was worthless. White men were notorious liars. What Stevens really had in mind was "relocation" to some awful desert where they would starve. The Chehalis, he said, would not participate.

The next day Stevens arrived for the treaty

signing. The Governor was drunk. He said sign the treaty. Tleyuk said he would not sign. The Governor said all the tribes would have to sign or there would be no treaty. Tleyuk refused. The Governor said, okay, not only is there no treaty but you aren't chiefs anymore, and he took away their chief's papers. This aggrieved them greatly.

The other tribes were eventually accommodated by other treaties, leaving the Cowlitz alone without a share of the salmon that had been theirs. There had been failed Cowlitz lawsuits before. But the Prettybirds, intent on justice, brought the issue before the court yet one more time. The Cowlitz chief had signed the treaty in good faith, they argued. He wasn't responsible for Tleyuk's stubbornness or Isaac Stevens' drunkenness.

When Rodney Prettybird cast his nets off the mouth of the Columbia, as he was licensed to do, he incurred the wrath of Doug Egan. Egan, who fished out of Astoria, on the Oregon side of the river, didn't like competition—especially Indians. The idea that Rodney was in court seeking a treaty share of the salmon infuriated him. He blamed the Native Americans for the decline in salmon stocks and had taken to "corking" Rodney Prettybird's nets—placing his nets in front of Rodney's to rob Rodney of his catch.

I said, "It could be Egan, too. Have you ever thought about that? It could be Egan."

"If Egan's the guy, I suppose I could understand why Rodney wants to take care of it himself. I would, too."

"Rodney's a Cowlitz who wants treaty rights. Maybe it is Egan," I said. "You have to consider all possibilities. We've got Mike Stark to think about. We've got Egan."

"Doug Egan doesn't give a damn about Melinda's love life. He just wants all the salmon."

"I think I should talk to Melinda some more. Hear what she has to say."

Willie took a sip of beer. "I'll give her a call and see if it's okay for us to drive on down now." He got up and went to the phone booth and was back in a couple of minutes. "Sure. No problem," he said. "Melinda says to come down. She'll tell you everything you want to know. She can handle it now. Prib's with her, so she's safe. I've mentioned Prib before, haven't I?"

"A couple of times."

"He's the bricklayer, guy I grew up with. We better get going." Willie Prettybird was a worried big brother. He had a right to be.

3 DISCOVERY IN THE PARK

A cold, wet mist rode a hard wind that swept in from Puget Sound as Willie Prettybird drove me to the Montana Verde apartments in south Seattle, where his sister lived. There were times, in weak moments, when I felt the weather in the Puget Sound should be included retroactively, in Hades, or purgatory, or wherever it is people are supposed to suffer for their sins. There were some politicians I could think of who should be made to pace the Seattle waterfront, naked save maybe for a few chains, for eternity. I had grown up in desert country in northeastern Oregon, where you could use a frozen cow pie for a discus in the winter and your feet stuck to asphalt streets in the summer. Now this. Was there no justice?

Willie Prettybird didn't think so. He got angrier and angrier as we drove through the rain, listening to the *click, click* of the windshield wipers. "You know it's not right, Denson, for a guy like Mike Stark to terrorize a woman. He's got bucks and he's a professor, so people say, hey, he's not the kind of screwball who'd beat up a woman. It's his word against a Cowlitz squaw."

"It's always best to keep a clear mind, Willie. All we're after is the truth so we can protect Melinda and keep Rodney out of trouble. How often does Rodney come to Seattle?"

Willie slowed for a stop light. "Not much. Maybe once a month, something like that. There's the Montana Verde up there on the left."

If I remembered my Spanish, Montana Verde meant green mountain. The architecture of the apartment complex was urban-renewal-utilitarian—or maybe poor-people-drab—as opposed to anything Spanish. Because of its location at the base of a ridge, the residents of the Montana Verde were blocked from seeing the Cascades, or even Mt. Rainier. Owing to a high-rise insurance building, they couldn't see the snow-capped Olympic range on the far side of the sound. In fact, the Montana Verde was probably the only apartment building in the Seattle area where clear days weren't blessed by a fabulous view of a mountain. This was a remarkable achievement by the developer.

A few miles south of the Montana Verde was the city of Renton, the suburban Seattle site of one of the Boeing Company's aerospace assembly plants—one of several in the Puget Sound area. Whether it made 747s or surface-to-air missiles, Boeing employed a lot of workers. When Boeing fell on hard times a few years back, someone erected a sign at the Seattle city limits saying the last person out of town should turn out the lights. But Boeing's fortunes prospered with President Reagan's decision to rebuild the military, and so did Seattle's.

The Montana Verde, probably built in the early 1960s, was the home of several hundred blue-collar workers and divorced women with children—women trying to make do on the salary of a receptionist or clerk and child support that might or might not be paid. It was hard to believe that Melinda, having come into a two-hundred-thousand-dollar divorce settlement, would turn her money over to fishing boats and legal fees and live in a place like this.

The asphalt on the apartment parking lot had long ago been destroyed by George's Cheap Mart oil dripping from the bottoms of old, large Buicks and Oldsmobiles—the kinds of "good transportation" that go for a few hundred bucks in a car lot. Several decrepit cars and pickup trucks, in such sorry shape that even the loan companies shunned them, had been abandoned in the lot. The decaying hulks were the bodies of dinosaurs too old and too slow to survive and so were stuck in a modern tar pit. That the Detroit engineers who designed them had brains the size of walnuts, I did not doubt.

There was a complicated tower of monkey bars in the center of the grassy area around the tar-pit parking lot. The grassy area was originally intended by a landscape architect to give the Montana Verde a touch of verde, but it had been pounded to hard, sour earth by the feet of running children.

Willie Prettybird parked his Toyota in a parking slot that was filthy from accumulated petroleum goo. Willie shook his head. "When we get the company turned around a little, I'm getting Melinda out of this fucking place."

Willie led me up the sidewalk toward the main entrance of the left side of a V-shaped apartment building. I stepped over a tricycle minus its front wheel and picked up the remains of a frisbee. The frisbee had once been part of a department-store promotion. Around the edges of the moon-shaped fragment was a promotion for something called the Puget Sound Value Days:

LIVE, IN PERSON, TOBY KN
OYS, JULY 15–17

I followed Willie through a large room intended for parties and large gatherings for residents of the Montana Verde. There were rips and tears in the plastic covers of the sofas and chairs in the commons.

"The elevator works but I like to walk," Willie said. He started up the concrete stairs. He took the stairs two at a time. He was light on his feet.

"Slow down, Willie."

Willie slowed. "By the way, Prib's real name's Gary. Rodney and I call him Prib, that's for priblige, on account of once when we were kids and'd had too much beer and were in the giggle stage, he managed to call himself a pribliged character. We called him Priblige for years, then we shortened it." Willie smiled at the memory of how the Pribliged Gary had become Priblige, then Prib.

I was starting to puff, thinking maybe I ought to lay off the mayonnaise and egg yolks.

Willie paused on the stairs. "Prib'll appreciate any chore you can give him, John. He gets pissed at people who mistreat Melinda." Willie started taking the stairs two at a time again.

"We'll see what happens," I said.

Willie Prettybird thumped cheerfully on the door of his sister's apartment. "Her damn bonger went out. I'm gonna have to fix it for her." He waited, and when there was no answer, he banged on the door with his fist. "Hey, Melinda!" he called.

There was no answer.

"Melinda!" he yelled. The color drained from Willie Prettybird's face. He banged again. He tried the door handle. Locked. He looked at me, panicked.

"Why don't you read the note?" I said.

"What note?" Willie looked wild-eyed.

"The one under the door there."

Willie, looking foolish, retrieved an envelope whose edge stuck out from under the door. He retrieved a slip of paper from the envelope and we both read it:

Dear Willie,
 Sorry to stand up you and your friend but

Prib had to go and I got scared here by myself. Don't blame Prib. My fault. I'll call you soon.

Melinda

Willie folded the note and tucked it into his wallet.

"Is that her handwriting?" I asked.

"It looks like it, but she could have written it with a knife at her throat. This isn't like her, Denson. She just wouldn't take off like this."

"She could have gotten scared like the note says."

"Where did she go?" Willie said. "She said to come right down. She said Prib was with her. Where did she go, Denson? Where?" With that the panicked Willie stepped back and rammed the door with his shoulder like in the movies.

"Hey! Hey! Whoa!" I said. "You're gonna hurt your shoulder for nothing." I retrieved my car keys from my pocket and unfolded a little tool from the ring that I used on the lock to Melinda's apartment door. "Lots easier this way, Willie." The lock clicked open and we stepped inside.

Melinda Prettybird's apartment looked orderly enough. There were no signs of violence. The top two drawers of her bureau were empty save for a bra with a broken strap. Her closet was mostly empty except for summer clothes. In the room where her two small sons slept, the winter clothes were also missing.

"Neat job of packing," I said. "That'd take a while."

Willie clenched his jaw. "Let's get out of here," he said.

"Do you know how to find Prib?"

"No," Willie said. He folded the letter and started down the stairs. Halfway down, he said, "Prib's been hanging out with Rodney lately. Maybe he's with Rodney."

The drains of the Montana Verde's parking lot were plugged and we had to wade back to Willie's car. We waited for the engine to warm and for the defogger to clear the windows. "If somebody was watching her, the stupidest thing she could do was take off like that," Willie said.

"Maybe she just got scared, like she said. If I were you, Willie, I'd get on the phone to the cops pronto."

"Police!" Willie was disgusted. "The cops come out to a place like this and their minds are half made up before they walk in the door."

"Those guys have to be careful. More people get hurt intervening in lovers' quarrels than any other kind of call."

"The cops find out Melinda's a Cowlitz and they think, oh, shit, Redskins."

Willie needed a break from my questions. I turned on the radio and picked up the Sonics in the fourth quarter in Los Angeles. It was early October and already the long season of the National Basketball Association was under way. The Sonics were up by four in a tight game; I listened to the game and left Willie to worry in peace. The Sonics held on to win by three and I turned the radio off.

The water on black asphalt made the streets mirrorlike, shiny, a little dangerous because they were both slick and hard to see. Willie slowed and checked his headlights to make sure they were on. Willie braked and swerved to avoid a VW that had pushed a yellow. Willie glared at the bug.

"When something like this happens to one of us, I mean like this guy beating up Melinda's boyfriends, why it's embarrassing. The police come out and talk to Melinda in that damn place back there, and what do they conclude? A squaw. Melinda doesn't have to live there, you know, she gives her money to the lawsuit same as Rodney and me. She's bright, besides being good-looking. But it's hard for any woman to have a social life when she has two children to take care of. What do you say let's finish the day off at the Pig's and join the wake. I can call the cops from there."

"Sounds like a deal to me," I said.

"I can't imagine the cops'll do any good," Willie said. He didn't have a whole lot of confidence in the local Forces of Good. He turned his car across town, toward the waterfront and the Pig's Alley.

There, arm-in-arm with our old friends, we got thoroughly sloshed and sentimental. The jazzmen played melancholy riffs with lips of midnight. We drank. We talked. We remembered. We sang songs. We were being evicted from our comfortable spot by Seattle's chi-chi crowd, and we resented it. The fashionables got first dibs on everything worthwhile but were too shallow, in our opinion, to appreciate anything except hot tubs and cars with silver paint. This sardonic view of life was no way diminished by the story carried from the streets by an inebriated messenger a half hour before closing time.

To the crew at the Pig's, the news was part of a faint whinnying that they had often discussed on long rainy afternoons. The whinnying somehow got louder each year. The horses were skittish as the riders of the apocalypse prepared to mount: The drunk said a large chunk of flesh from a still-warm human corpse had been found inside Pioneer Place Park down on First Avenue; it was on the radio.

4 KILLERS

On Saturday, our last night at the Pig's Alley—
with sentiment pouring as freely as the Rainier
and Henry Weinhard's—Federal Judge Moby
Rappaport joined Melinda Prettybird on Seattle's missing-persons list.

The Pig's was chaos in its dying hours. Some
of the regulars, stoned on southern Oregon
bud, listened to the Irish folk singers honored
with the last gig at the Pig's and reminisced
about characters they had known and women
they had met in the Pig's. These conversations
usually led to a consideration of a former
habitué of the Pig's, a construction worker
named William DuPreis, Bill to us, who an-
nounced one afternoon that he had begun taking hormone shots and was going to have his
weasel surgically removed so that he could become Wilma. Some patrons watched a Clint
Eastwood movie on the tube above the bar. It
didn't matter to the Dirty Harry fans that they
couldn't hear the dialogue; they cheered enthu-
siastically whenever Eastwood blew away a
jerk with his .44 Magnum. A few couples—

caught up by the sentiment of the occasion—pawed one another in steamy closeness.

Some of us played darts, remembering how it was in the days we had won some of the Pig's house trophies that now collected dust on a shelf above the bar.

I had arrived early, hoping to get a shot at the chair that was the prize of Pig's Alley. The chairs at the Pig's were so scarred and carved up, so old and corroded by accumulations of sweat, beer, and smoke, that they were worthless on the market. It was understood by the owner and the Pig's regulars that there would be none remaining at closing. The prize chair was one in which a failed pornographic artist had once committed suicide by ramming a knife into his stomach, hara-kiri–style.

When I stepped through the door, the rotund Stan, owner of the Pig's, got up from the chair to help with a faulty beer keg. All right! I thought. I slipped my jacket over the back of the chair and left a half-empty glass of beer on the seat every time I left it to go to the john.

All of the regular dart players of the Pig's were there and feeling good. There was Mike Odell, Captain Mikey. Mike Scanlan, Scabby, originally Scablan, famous for his wretched sevens and elevens. Ron Cardinal, Rodent Clone—sometimes R. C. Darryl Bean, the Beaner, known for his scores of twenty-four, called Beaners by those who knew him. There was Willie, of course, Chief Dumbshit, and me, the Natural Assholete and Master of Zen Darts.

We shot for the bull's-eye to see who got to name the game. I slipped my quarter into the ashtray that banked the pot and took my shot. My dart wound up alone in the double-bull. I chose Killer, which was what we called it when there were women present. Otherwise it was Fuck Your Buddy. It was a simple game: you set the number which has your three lives by throwing at the board with your off hand; once you hit the double of your own number you're a killer and can throw at the doubles of your opponents; each time your number is struck, it's a life—three lives and you're dead.

Killer is especially amusing because it sets players against one another—some players are uncertain, some cunning, some brazen. The usual strategy was for weaker players to gang up on the stronger. Stronger players sometimes combat this by forming an alliance of their own. When this happens weaker players deny being any part of a conspiracy. Character is revealed.

"Asshole," Rodent Clone said, when I called Killer.

"That's the way the mop flops," said Captain Mikey.

Willie and I kept our eye on the tube because the Sonics were winning in Los Angeles and there would be highlights following the game. Willie was a passionate Sonics fan. He was also the best player in a game of Killer, and so the rest of us conspired to get him first.

Willie grumbled at the dubious honor of

having to defend himself first. After him we'd go for Captain Mikey, Scabby, or the Rodent Clone, depending on how their games were going. My strategy was to lay low and repeat how I was the worst player in the pot, a threat to no one. I ran my private-eye business pretty much the same way. The Beaner made crass wisecracks, aimed equitably at everyone in turn.

Willie adjusted his flights. It was his turn. "Ever since this happened to Melinda I've been thinking Cochise, Geronimo." He stepped up to the line and fired at my number—*thump! thump! thump!*—taking two of my allotted three lives, and walked away, grinning triumphantly.

"Hey, why crap on me?" I said. "What about Captain Mikey or the Scab?"

Rodent Clone said, "Because he doesn't go along with your game of turning us against one another while you stand there with that stupid grin on your face."

"Hey! C'mon," I said.

Scabby said, "Denson sort of looks like a dog eating manure. Did you ever notice that?"

"Mr. Zen Darts!" Rodent Clone made a farting sound with his tongue and lower lip and dug at an itch on the inside of his thigh.

The set was turned up to full volume to compete with the band, the singing, and the drunken shouting. The Sonics were off to a fast start—they had beaten both Philadelphia and Boston on the road, an amazing feat. In view of their dreadful finish the previous year, it was a miracle on the order of raising Lazarus from the dead. The television people knew this, of course, and tantalized us with upcoming highlights of the Sonics' win, forcing us to watch people arguing with one another and shooting one another in an effort to be given star listing on the playbill and to remain center stage.

The silver-haired anchorman told us about how there was fear we were going to get sucked into a war in the Middle East. Then his woman partner told us about a famous actress who had died in Hollywood and left her estate to a cat. The silver-haired man looked grim during the Middle East story. The woman tried to look amused by the actress story.

"Come on, for Christ's sake," Willie said. He wanted to see Jack Sikma putting it to the aging Jabbar.

"We'll be right back with a story about a missing federal judge," the woman said. "Highlights of the Sonics' victory coming up."

"Which is all we give a damn about, lady," muttered the mighty Captain Mikey. Odell was an accountant who always double-checked the score to make sure it was right. He hit Scabby for one of the Scab's lives and giggled.

"Nice guy," Scanlan said. He stepped to the line and fired at the Captain's number.

Listening to this chatter, Willie and I waited our turns at the board and talked about his sister's disappearance. "You can bet the cops'll do their damnedest to find a federal judge," Willie said bitterly. That morning Willie had gone back to the Montana Verde with the police so detectives could search her apartment. They called him back later in the day to say they had no leads but were still looking.

There were advertisements for light beer, dog food, and mouth wash, after which the silver-haired man was back:

"Federal Judge Moby Rappaport was reported missing today after he failed to return from a Justice Department meeting in San Francisco. The police say Rappaport was scheduled to return to Seattle yesterday afternoon. Judge Rappaport was to have ruled next week on a controversial suit filed by the Cowlitz Indians to be included among tribes enjoying treaty fishing rights. Here is Saundra Nordquist in Ilwaco, where residents were upset by the possibility of Cowlitz fishermen being awarded a court-ordered share of the salmon entering the Columbia River."

"What? Rappaport?" Prettybird's head jerked. "What's this?"

"Missing yesterday. Just like Melinda," I said.

Beaner said, "Your turn, Dumbshit."

Willie took three shots that sailed way wide of Rodent Clone's number, which wasn't smart because R. C. was clearly in a slump. Willie's third shot was so wild it clunked against the wall. That wasn't the form that made him the dominant player of the Pig's Alley.

When he got back, it was clear Willie could hardly believe the news. "Two years of legal fees and the judge is missing. That's a lot of wampum, Denson."

Another blond woman, younger and maybe not as pretty as the anchorwoman, was now on the television screen. She stood on the docks at Ilwaco—a fishing village at the mouth of the Columbia River. A hard wind pressed against her yellow rainslicker. "George, I have here William 'Foxx' Jensen, spokesman for the Northwest Sport Fishermen's Association, which has been following this case closely."

"He owns a bar and motel in Ilwaco, the bastard," Willie said.

Foxx Jensen was a middle-aged man with a slight paunch, close-cropped hair, and bushy eyebrows. He stood in front of the camera wearing a green-and-red-checked wool shirt. There was an adoring dog by his side—a German shorthair. He looked solemn. "Of course, we're all concerned about Judge Rappaport's disappearance. As you know, he was about to give a decision in the Cowlitz Indian lawsuit, and we're all anxious to bring this thing to a close."

The camera cut to the reporter, who peered earnestly from under the hood of the yellow rainslicker. "Do you have any idea of how the judge was leaning on the Cowlitz case?" she asked.

"Well," Jensen said, "I don't think there's any question how the issue will eventually be decided. We have ample evidence that the Columbia River salmon run is overfished as it is. Restoring treaty fishing rights to a tribe that never had them in the first place is both illogical and contrary to common sense. I can't imagine the courts seeing it any other way." Jensen sounded reasonable. He was a reasonable man, his attitude said, not a greedy Redskin.

Willie Prettybird said, "Bullshit. Where the hell's Janine? Why doesn't she have her brains and cute butt up there to put that asshole in his place?"

"You have a woman lawyer?" I said.

The reporter in Ilwaco said Janine Hallen, attorney for the Cowlitz plaintiffs in the case, was out of town and not available for comment.

The silver-haired anchorman was back on the screen again, saying that Rappaport's law clerk, Kim Hartwig, fresh out of Georgetown University Law School, was also reported missing, but the police did not know if the disappearances were related.

"God, Denson, if something happened to Rappaport, we'll draw Awdrey. Ain't no way we can afford Awdrey. No way!"

"Who's Awdrey?"

"Judge Louise Awdrey. Janine says all the lawyers call her John Wayne."

"John Wayne?"

"On account she likes to blow Redskins off their ponies. Hates us. Thinks we're worthless drunks."

"Oh, boy."

"We get Awdrey and Janine'll have to build our case all over again, from scratch. Janine says you have to play the judge. You have to know what they like and don't like; judges're all different."

"Hah, the Natural Assholete takes the big banana!" Darryl Bean pulled his darts, the last of which was stuck in the double fourteen, my last life. I was out of the game.

"Being a nice guy won't save you, Beaner." Captain Mikey stepped up and began throwing at the double-two, Bean's life.

The bartender said Willie had a phone call. While Willie talked on the phone, glancing in my direction a couple of times, I watched Dr. Ralph's eleven o'clock version of more rain tomorrow and waited for the Sonics highlights. This was the longest-running show in Seattle. Just what the rotund Ralph was a doctor of was uncertain. He could have been a philosopher or chiropractor, for all the public knew. The implication was that he was a meteorologist and so had some kind of inside track on more rain.

Ralph used his pointer on a satellite photograph provided by the National Weather Service. He told us all what we already knew: that those clouds over the Pacific were headed straight for us, as usual, and it was going to keep on raining. "There was a high of eighty-seven in French Lick, Indiana, today," Dr. Ralph said. He looked naughty.

Willie Prettybird returned from the phone looking shaken. "That was my neighbor," he said.

"Let me guess. The police came calling," I said.

"They were asking questions about me."

"They want to talk to you about Moby Rappaport, I'll bet."

"We're the last people, the absolute rock-bottom last people to suspect of anything stupid, Denson. It was going our way. There was no question, none, that we would have gotten treaty rights next week. How else could it have gone? How else? It was going our way, no question."

"You couldn't possibly know that for sure."

"It was going our way. Besides, do we need to draw Awdrey? That'd be like peeing in the pemmican."

Ron Cardinal took Willie Prettybird's last life. "Takes care of the Native American," the Rodent Clone smirked.

Willie laughed. "Sure, sure. Another Redskin bites the dust."

"Way the world works," said Rodent Clone.

Willie and I were no longer killers. The remaining players paused momentarily to assess the board and decide how to draw blood without inspiring retaliation.

"You never know how cops think," I said. "That guy on the tube there, Jensen or whatever his name is, he thought Rappaport was leaning the other direction."

Willie scowled. "He's full of it up to his eyebrows, too."

"That woman they were talking about on the tube, your lawyer. What's her name?"

"Janine."

"Yes, Janine. Does she do criminal work too?"

"What do you mean by that?"

"I mean, it's just possible that the cops are taking a good hard look at you and Rodney. A federal judge is missing. People are going to want to know what happened to him."

Willie turned angry. "Fuck Judge Rappaport. I want to know what happened to Melinda Prettybird."

The whole darts crew vowed to find another place to throw so they could continue playing Killer on Sunday afternoons.

"We'll find a place," Captain Mikey said.

Scabby said, "There'll be a place."

When at last Stan said it was, irrevocably, time to close the doors, I rose with the rest, my suicide chair in hand.

Stan said, "You didn't have to nail your ass to the damned thing, Denson, it was yours all along."

"What?"

Willie said, "Stan here passed the word early in the evening. We all decided it should be yours."

Stan laughed. "Dumb asshole."

I was pleased at their thoughtfulness. It was a wonderful gesture. "Thank you both," I said. I held the chair up for them to admire. "Just the right size for my breakfast nook. I can sit there and contemplate broken yolks."

5 THE DOIE

None of us had recovered from our hangovers the next day before workmen began gutting the interior of the Pig's Alley to make way for Le Cuisine de Pacifique. Melinda Prettybird had now been missing for almost two days, and Judge Moby Rappaport was missing as well. Willie repeatedly called a friend of Melinda's in Scappose, Oregon, thinking she might be there. No answer. He tried again and again to call his brother, Rodney, in Astoria, Oregon. No answer.

Willie Prettybird said he maybe understood how the salmon felt when the white man built a string of twenty-eight dams on the Columbia River, yes, twenty-eight, and in the process destroyed the largest salmon run in the world. There was nowhere else for them to go. For that matter, there was no place for us. Where were we going to rendezvous, Willie and me? Where were we going to throw darts and talk about the Sonics' new look and about how hard it was to get laid?

With Melinda Prettybird missing we forgot about the Sonics and getting laid. We needed a bar where we could meet during our investigation.

We both assumed that we would find a new place together. That we might go our separate ways, find new partners for darts, was unthinkable. Willie knew all the weaknesses of my game. When I pressed and began to lift my left foot, he'd tell me to get it back on the floor. When I shot too rapidly, he'd tell me to slow down. He was quicker with numbers than I was. When the pressure was on I could depend on him to be there behind me, saying softly, "Trip fourteen, double sixteen," or "trip seventeen, double top"—whatever strategy or the odds dictated—so that I could concentrate on the board. When I was down to outs, he'd say, "Zen darts, John. Take your time. Zen darts," and I'd slip into my trance.

Whenever Willie jerked his hand or let his elbow float, I'd let him know. Whenever he started making a little rolling motion with his body, I'd tell him to knock it off.

I tried to call Mike Stark at home and at the history department at the University of Washington, but he was at neither place. There wasn't a lot I could do about Melinda until I talked to Stark, so Willie and I decided to search for another bar with boards. We cruised up and down First and Second looking for a place without derelicts or affected worshipers of the buck.

Late that afternoon we stepped into Juantar's

Doie Bar, a small place on Yesler Way directly across from Pioneer Place Park, where the chunk of human flesh had been found the night of Melinda's disappearance. The man behind the bar had the grin of a mischievous imp. He had green eyes and curly blond hair, thin on top, and an equally curly beard. He was nervous. He was a pacer.

"Ah, pigeons. Gentlemen, gentlemen, can I help you?" he said in a Southern drawl.

Willie and I ordered beer and looked around, casing the Doie.

The Southerner noticed this. "You'll find folks here in the Doie're comfortable with the smell of human sweat," he said. "They've known the highs and lows of human experience. I've got alcoholic talkers, failed intellectuals, bicycle riders, readers of arcane science fiction, numerologists, scatologists, hang gliding enthusiasts, and cribbage players. There're no snitches or narcs that I know of. Name's Juantar Chauvin. The drawl's Bayou."

Willie and I introduced ourselves, simultaneously spotting the Doie's dart boards.

"How is it you passed on pool tables and video games?" I asked.

"Can't stand 'em," Juantar said. "Dart boards are okay. If they made a racket, I wouldn't have 'em around."

Thus it was that Willie Prettybird and I found our place.

"We'll have to tell Scab and Rodent Clone."

"I agree," Willie said. "Didn't this used to be the Evergreen Bar?" he asked Juantar.

"Used to be," Juantar said. "There was a hotel here before that. I used to be a lawyer, but I got bored with all those details. Wanted to have me some fun." Juantar grinned. "I bought this place sight unseen from a trade magazine."

Willie said, "There was a hotel here before that."

"Built directly over a Chinese whorehouse that used to operate out of the basement. Let me show you something." Juantar retrieved a couple of brass tokens the size of silver dollars from a bowl up behind the bar. They were from "The China Doll," a Wild West brothel in Dodge City. Juantar showed Willie and me one of the tokens. The prices listed on the tokens were the source of the name of Juantar's Doie Bar:

10 CENTS LOOKIE / 25 CENTS FEELIE / 50 CENTS DOIE

"You get what you pay for. Praise Jesus!" Juantar said. He rubbed one of the tokens with his thumb. "See here, doie. You live once. If you don't get a little doie, why bother? You rub it with your thumb and it'll bring you luck and much doie. See here." He rubbed it with his thumb. He reached up behind the bar and took two more tokens from another bowl. They were duplicates of the China Doll tokens, only on the back they said, "Juantar's Doie Bar,

Seattle, WA." He gave each of us a token. "Now if you ever get in a jam and need a little luck, why then you just rub your token with your thumb. If you don't want to lose it, you can drill a hole in it if you want and hang it on your keychain."

I slipped my token into my pocket. I've never been particularly superstitious, but the truth is the token was comforting for some curious reason. I had it in my pocket if I needed it.

It was then that I noticed the cardboard silhouettes behind the bar, labeled "folk dancers."

"Those bullet holes?" I asked.

"Yup," Juantar said. "I change the label every once in a while to give my customers something to talk about. There's a bunch of folk dancers hoppin' around at the Seattle Center this week." Juantar looked proudly at his silhouettes.

"A national convention, according to the paper," Willie said.

"I drive out to a gravel pit and practice with my pistol on weekends. I call my silhouettes liberals, feminists, Republicans, Protestants, or vegetarians. Whatever. I especially like conventions of people who walk around with plastic name tags on their lapels." Juantar grinned. "I find it amusing when folks tighten their lips."

Juantar Chauvin might have been superstitious about rubbing his doie token, but judging from his cynical use of Christian exclamations and exhortations, he didn't have a religious bone in his body. That afternoon he interrupted the Doie's reggae to play tapes of evangelical preachers. "This is for the amusement of the house," Juantar said in his Bayou drawl. "We listen to old Jim Bakker and maybe the rain'll go away. Praise the Lord!"

A man in a business suit or in a blazer and neat tie was a secret object of disdain in the Doie, as was the woman on the make for a man with a bottomless wallet. Juantar said the chic set understood this and avoided the bar.

Willie and I found the regulars at the Doie to be congenially eccentric; they were amused by the dramatic histrionics of evangelist preachers and Juantar's outrageous commentary on the mentality of the herd in all its human forms. We fit right in, as comfortable as we had been in the Pig's Alley.

Willie and I stayed until closing that first night.

We were talking about Melinda Prettybird and playing a dart game called Fifty-five Fives, when Juantar came over to tell us that October was a month of anticipation at the Doie.

"Halloween's Frighten Your Neighbor night," he said. "I talk it up all month long. Y'all'll find that out. The Doie sits right square over the Seattle underground, do you know that? Do you? There're spookies and boogies down there, ghosts, dead men in chains, virgins who cry by night—right out of old Edgar Allan himself. You can't miss it! You can't!"

"Sounds like real fun," Willie said.

Juantar said, "Oh, yes, Willie, we'll all have fun. Everybody'll have a good time on Halloween. It's Frighten Your Neighbor night at the Doie." Juantar squirmed with anticipation.

6 STARK'S STORY

The next morning—posing as a magazine salesman—I called Professor Michael Stark at home. He was there, but wasn't interested in magazines. It's always a mistake to warn someone by telephone if you suspect they won't want to talk to you, so I drove unannounced to Michael Stark's house, a restored 1940s bungalow at the edge of the U-District. The house had a quiet, contemplative look about it, nestled there under large elms. The back yard opened into a park that sloped down into a ravine. I could see joggers in colorful outfits on a trail far below.

Out front sat a bright red 1939 Ford coupe, a beautiful car.

I whacked the door twice with a hinged brass knocker in the shape of a naked lady working her legs. Mike Stark answered the door, wearing a dark blue Amsterdam Hard Rock Café T-shirt with a red marijuana leaf on it. He was a short man with a black beard and mischievous brown eyes. He was smoking a neatly rolled joint.

"May I help you?" Stark asked. He looked quizzical. He made no effort to hide the joint, which he held between his thumb and forefinger, his little pinkie in the air.

"Well," I said. "My name is John Denson; I'm a private investigator here in the Seattle area. I'm looking into the disappearance of Judge Moby Rappaport. I'm told you were scheduled to appear as an expert witness in the Cowlitz fishing rights case."

"Private investigator? I've already talked to the police."

"Judge Rappaport held a life-insurance policy. His wife is the beneficiary."

"Oh, oh, I see. I'll be glad to answer your questions, Mr. Denson, although I don't think I can add anything to what I've already told the police." Stark took a hit on his joint and giggled. "Good thing you aren't a narc, isn't it? The Cowlitz are a lovely people. Listen, I've got something I want you to see. Come on in here and take a look." He handed me the joint, as if there were no doubt but that I smoked pot.

"Thanks." I took a toke to be friendly and followed him across the polished hardwood floor into an earthen-colored, tiled kitchen with handsome enameled cookware hanging from wooden hooks on the ceiling.

But the centerpiece, what Stark wanted to show me, was piled on top of a newspaper in the center of the cherrywood kitchen table. Stark stood by the table and grinned hugely, grinned proudly. "Aren't they wonderful? They're wonderful. Aren't they beauties? Aren't they? Look at 'em. Fat babies. *Cantharellus cibarius.*"

Cantharellus cibarius was apparently the Latin name for some apricot-colored mushrooms on the newspaper. Vertical wavy gills ran down much of the length of the stem, getting wider as the mushrooms blossomed out at the top. "Impressive," I said.

"You bet. Chanterelles. They're delicious. The Pacific Northwest is marvelous for mushroom hunting, marvelous. All this rain—once in a while we get a little sun. Have you ever eaten Chanterelles, Mr. Denson?"

"Well, no, I haven't."

"Let me fry us some in a little butter while we talk. There are thousands more where those come from. They're delicious, you'll see. The French have orgasms at the very thought of them. The ones you buy in stores are *Agaricus bisphorus. Agaricus pissporus,* I call 'em." Stark took another hit on his joint and set about cutting up some Chanterelles on a butcher-block table mounted on casters. Stark was quick with a knife: chop-chop-chop, chop-chop-chop. "I used to be married to a Cowlitz, do you know that, Mr. Denson? The jolly Jew and his Indian wife. Woo, woo, woo!" Stark did a parody of an Indian dance as he chopped mushrooms. "Melinda Prettybird, her name is. Cute? Is she cute? She has these eyes. Oh, my man!"

I didn't say anything. Better to let him talk. Stark seemed not to know Melinda was missing, but I knew better than to accept anything he said at face value. Neurotics make good liars. If he was as crazy as Willie said, he was capable of anything.

"You must never believe anything a Cowlitz says about me, Mr. Denson. Melinda and I had an ugly parting, and there were claims made." Stark smiled. "The Cowlitz hang together; I'll give them that. Fish stories. Do you know what a fish story is?" He flopped a wad of butter, *plup*, in a cast iron skillet.

"Oh, sure."

"I suppose everybody has told one at least once in his life. Looking back, the fish look a little bigger, don't they? They fought a little harder. There were a few more of them. I guess most fish stories are harmless enough. But you need to be careful, Mr. Denson. How about some coffee while these cook? Little caffeine'll do us good." He poured us each a cup. "Smell these babies. Just smell 'em."

I inhaled deeply. "Oh, boy!"

Stark set about rolling another joint. "Melinda has this way of looking you straight on with those brown eyes of hers and lying like hell. Have you met her? Have you? Have you seen those eyes? She pulled that stunt with the divorce judge, you know, called me every name in the book going blink, blink, blink all the while. God, what I wouldn't have given for a woman judge."

"Turned your wallet over to her, I take it."

"I think she married me mostly because I

had inherited a few bucks. She didn't want to run around in the mountains looking for mushrooms. She was into things, man. She loved the feel of a credit card, loved it; I think it made her nips turn hard. She hit me for two-hundred grand when we split. I knew I'd been had the second she walked into the courtroom. She looked like Sacajawea."

"So what do you think about Rappaport's disappearance, Mr. Stark?"

"I don't have any idea. Listen, on that business with my ex-wife. The police have sworn affadavits on my whereabouts on each occasion. I assure you, the administration at the university would frown on one of its professors lying under oath, much less beating up on people. I'm a scholar, not a thug. I write articles for journals nobody reads. Besides that, I had witnesses, man, witnesses." Stark slid a couple of plates on the table along with some forks. "It's hard for me to believe Willie would even think of doing anybody harm. Rodney, now, he's something else. That man has a temper."

"I have to admit I thought it was a far-fetched idea to begin with, but if I don't ask all the questions the insurance people'll want to know why."

Stark stirred the frying mushrooms with a wooden spoon. "Melinda Prettybird would never give big bucks to a lawsuit and live in the Montana Verde unless there were bucks at the end of the march. I suppose you have to check everything out. There are a number of people who would have benefited from Moby Rappaport's death. It all depends . . .''

"On what?"

"On your reading of his comments in court and the questions Rappaport asked of the various attorneys involved. There's a lot of money to be won or lost in any salmon decision, depending on how the courts divvy the fish. If you're trying to make sense out of the salmon-fishing industry, you have to understand the economics. If the Prettybirds win their lawsuit, they get treaty rights to salmon entering the Columbia. The salmon have to go up the Columbia to get to the Cowlitz."

"And Doug Egan wouldn't like that."

"Doug Egan's the biggest commercial fisherman in Astoria. His boats fish out of the Columbia. The Prettybirds are ordinary commercial competition now, but give them treaty rights and they're another kind of competition entirely. They can take a court-ordered treaty share to the bank to borrow money for more boats."

"I can't imagine Egan wants more boats in the water."

"There are only so many fish to be had, Mr. Denson."

"And Judge Rappaport was about to do what?"

Stark looked surprised. He used the wooden spoon to slide the sautéed mushrooms onto our plates. "Why nobody knows! Judges have clerks do their research for them and sometimes even draft opinions. That's a lot of influence, man, a lot of influence. I have graduate assistants who help me with my work. When I'm writing an article, they know pretty much what I'm thinking. As long as judges have clerks, there's a possibility of leaks."

"So who stood to win or lose?"

"They all stand to gain; they all stand to lose—it depends. I'm talking all of them: seiners, gillnetters, trollers, sportsmen, Indians. You're talking about a lot of money, hundreds of thousands of dollars. Personally, I'd like to see the Prettybirds win their case. What's fair is fair. My being divorced from Melinda doesn't have anything to do with it. Willie's a good guy, though. It's hard not to like Willie. Aren't these good? Yummy!"

"Delicious," I said. That was no lie.

Stark was pleased. "Willie Prettybird really loved to hunt wild mushrooms, you know. I got him all turned on and he was good at it. Got himself a microscope so he could check spore prints, the works. I can find six or eight different kinds of edible mushrooms within a few hundred yards of here. Those babies love all this rain. You can find a couple kinds of *Boletus*, including *mirabilis* and *edulus;* two or three kinds of *Suillus;* you can find Cow Mushrooms, Chicken of the Woods, Lion's Mane, a couple of different coral mushrooms, Spreading Hedgehogs, these Chanterelles, of course."

Stark looked happy. "And that's not to mention Morels in the springtime."

"These sure are good." I decided I'd have to get Willie to teach me about mushrooms.

"Say, Mr. Denson, if you should happen to talk to any of the Prettybirds in your investigation, I do wish you would take anything they say about me with the proverbial grain of salt. You'll find Melinda Prettybird to be a lively, charming young woman. A beauty. But she's also a skillful, unconscionable liar. A liar like you just can't imagine. You must believe me." He paused. "There's one other thing I should tell you, I suppose, since we did bring it up and all. I said a judge's clerks tend to be the most frequent source of judicial leaks—this goes all the way to clerks of the Supreme Court, by the way . . ."

"And?"

"Well, I don't know if it's worth anything. It's probably nothing, but I was down at Ivar's a couple of weeks ago having some oyster stew. And do you know Doug Egan was there eating fried razor clams and having a little tête-à-tête with a young man I know to be a law clerk to Moby Rappaport. You know, I think it was that young man who is missing. I can't remember his name. Hartung. Hartburn. Something like that."

"Hartwig."

"Yes, Hartwig. Interesting." Mike Stark bunched his face in a merry grin. His eyes danced and teased. "I just love gossip, don't you? I just bet Doug Egan paid for the clerk's razor clams; those things are so damned expensive. Both a judge and his law clerk are missing. Isn't it fun to speculate, Mr. Denson? I bet that's why you're a detective." Stark took a long, deep hit on his joint. "God, aren't these mushrooms great? I know where I can get these big old *Boletus edulus*. Ceps, the French call them. Fat mothers. They make wonderful soup."

Mike Stark certainly didn't seem like the kind of guy who would run around threatening women, but then, as I learned long ago, a case like this was like playing Killer: I couldn't trust anybody.

7 WARRIORS

It was impossible to hang out at the Doie without considering that thing at the base end of Pioneer Place Park. When I first moved to Seattle, I thought it was a gazebo. I knew what a gazebo was—or thought I did—because I had seen the movie with Walter Slezak when I was a kid. The residents of Seattle called it a pergola, however, possibly as a challenge to people who don't do crossword puzzles. I had to look the word up, same as everybody else. My dictionary says a pergola is: 1. an arbor formed of horizontal trelliswork supported on columns or posts, over which vines or other plants are trained; 2. a colonnade having the form of such an arbor.

The Pioneer Place pergola fits definition two. I suppose it's difficult in these days of municipal labor unions to hire people with the background necessary to train vines to grow over a trellis. Besides that, there's all the expense of maintenance. Anyway, Pioneer Place is located at the intersection of First Avenue and Yesler Way, the southern end of Seattle's mean street, if by that you're talking about a city's inevitable avenue of tattoo parlors, hookers, and skin flicks. In contrast to the emotional thicket of First Avenue sleaze, the tiny patch of grass at Pioneer Place is a rose.

Alaskan Way is Seattle's waterfront street, and reckoning from there to the interior of the city, to the sterile obelisks of the international style of architecture, the avenues run north and south—parallel to the water. They're numbered after Alaskan Way, lowest numbers closest to the water. The Pig's Alley had been located near the intersection of First Avenue and Pike Street. The triangle-shaped Pioneer Place was nine blocks south of the market—where First turns to the southwest following the curve of the harbor.

The apex of the small triangle—which was bordered by a wrought-iron fence maybe thirty inches high—faced north, up the avenue of lost dreams. This apex was marked by a fifty-foot totem pole with winged turquoise and black figures sitting butt on head and facing Canada. The pergola, built along the base of the triangle, faced Juantar's Doie Bar, and five blocks behind that—to the south—the Kingdome.

The pergola was made of jet-black iron strips and had glass on top rather than vines. The columns, made of vertical metal lattice, were open and airy, made to suggest Victorian imitations of classical Roman architecture. The cornice of each column, which held the weight of marble in the Doric originals, was in this case

metal strips peeled back like wood before a
carver's knife or curls of apple skin. Somehow,
I always expected to see corseted Victorian
ladies sitting on the bench under the shelter of
the glass top—ladies with delicate parasols and
wide-brimmed hats, and an artist, maybe, wearing a neat little beret.

But no. The dispossessed and heavy-drinking
Native Americans of Seattle apparently identified with the totem pole, because the small
triangle of grass that was Pioneer Place was
their spot, at least unofficially. The pergola,
with its dry bench, was their refuge. They
gathered there to drink fortified screw-top, the
cheapest firewater available. Although I'll pass
on port or madeira, I have to say that my taste,
too, runs to screw-top. Many's the night I've
contemplated the city lights over a jug of Mr.
Gallo's zinfandel. I'm always suspect of people
who say they love opera or really can tell the
difference between one expensive wine and the
next. The gentlemen in the shelter of the
pergola were out to get sloshed, which is more
honest than a man with pointy-toed shoes
using a bottle of thirty-dollar Bordeaux to
impress a blond with green Maybelline on her
eyelids.

Having called them Native Americans, I'll
back off a bit and say I usually call them
Indians. There is a reason for this. Years ago, I
was the first reporter on the *Honolulu Star-
Bulletin* to get away with using Black rather
than Negro in a story. I called Stokey Car-

michael a black because he told me that's what he wanted. His desire was fine by me, although judging from the reaction of my city editor, you'd have thought I'd tried to torch him with napalm. When Willie Prettybird asked for the same consideration, I could hardly say no. Willie Prettybird called a bathroom a toilet. He called a custodian a janitor. In his opinion the term Native American was mostly insisted upon by breast-beaters who sang folk songs and drove Renaults. Willie said the folks under the pergola most likely called themselves Indians, although this was changing in some quarters. As for him, he said, "Call me a 'Native American' and I'll cut your tongue out, white man." Thus it was that around Willie Prettybird, at least, I stuck to calling Native Americans plain old Indians.

The Indians wore rumpled, undistinguished old trousers, Goodwill ski jackets, and woolen stocking caps to their powwows in the shelter of the pergola. The stocking caps took the edge off the wind.

Since poverty and alcoholism are color-blind, I suppose there should be more mixing of races on First Avenue than in other parts of Seattle. The fact is that even there the ideal was elusive—have-nots were as conscious of race as the haves. Given their druthers, blacks somehow found blacks, whites preferred whites. A Native American was most comfortable with a fellow Redskin.

The gentlemen of the bottle who made their

rendezvous at the First Avenue bench were
part of the white man's legacy; their nineteenth-
century ancestors suddenly had alcohol thrust
upon them. They had not had their systems
inured by centuries of drinking, as had the
French trappers, British traders, and American
settlers.

The men who gathered there—the Pergola
Warriors, Willie called them—turned to their
spot out of instinct, it seemed, as though they
were hankering for something under it, something in the soil, perhaps, maybe something
that had been covered over by the city. They
were under the shelter of the pergola all day
long, in groups of two or three. But at about
eleven at night, they began to gather in larger
numbers, moving through the shadows of the
street, bottles of port or muscatel in paper
bags. They stood and talked quietly, one foot
on the bench, paper bags in hand, or sat,
staring at the ground, paper bags between
their feet. They powwowed. They discussed the
day's adventures, assessing wounds with a shake
of the head. They smoked the peace pipe—
Prince Albert or Velvet, hand rolled, or a joint
if they could come by one. They drank. They
listened to the city. They watched people come
and go on the sidewalk. The city grew around
them and closed out their past.

The Indians at First Avenue and Yesler Way
were out of sight and so out of mind, except by
cops and social workers and folks on their way
to see a ballgame at the Kingdome. Local

newspaper editors, o.d.'d on the subject, as-
signed a feature on the park's inhabitants once
a year. The assignment was most often given to
someone new on the staff, a woman preferably,
so that the story would be liberal and poignant
and so nonracist.

The latest feature was an advance on a rally
and fund-raiser for various Native American
causes. In order to extend the interest beyond
the hard core who already knew about and
were concerned with Indian problems, the organizers added Indian storytellers to the program, which was to be held on Halloween day.
The storytellers, according to posters in bars
and coffeehouses across the city, would talk
about Coyote, who could change himself into a
man if necessary to teach the ways of the
animal people. There was first the Great Spirit,
the posters said, then the animal people.

One of the Indians interviewed by the
newspaper reporter said Coyote lived in the
desert country south of Hanford, where they
built reactors in World War II to provide fuel
for the first atomic bombs. When Coyote
appeared as a man, he said, he wore a red
bandana around his neck.

The regulars must have been amused by the
article. A few weeks later I noticed that red
bandanas had become fashionable at the bench-
side powwows. Even better was when I learned
that Willie Prettybird was among the list of
storytellers. Willie said he was going to tell a
Coyote story told to him by his grandmother.

"Well, hell, Willie," I said. "You're going to have to wear a red bandana. Dress for the occasion."

Willie laughed. "I'm way ahead of you on that one. They had 'em on sale over at Sears. Just the deal."

Juantar got all excited when he heard about Willie's red bandana. "An Indian god!" he exclaimed. He wiggled and shook and did a little dance. "Oh, Willie, you must wear your bandana to the Doie on Halloween. You must! You must! An Indian god! The women will go for that, Willie, better than a halfback for the Seahawks. Ghosts of hookers past will come up from the underground, and we'll sport and gambol like satyrs. You'll get all the porking you can handle, Willie, wait and see."

8 UNDERGROUND

It was Juantar Chauvin's opinion that the chunk of human flesh found behind the pergola was a sign the spookies were restless in the underground. "They're gonna dance with us," he said. "Gonna drink human blood." The streets surrounding the diminutive park were part of a fascinating and mostly forgotten underground city that was one of those curious accidents of history. In fact, the Chinese brothel that had once existed in the basement of the building where Juantar established the Doie was part of the underground. The reason for the existence of the labyrinth of subterranean sidewalks and rooms had to do with sewage. If Mariner batters in the nearby Kingdome had had a hard time adjusting to the curve ball, that wasn't anything compared to the anguish suffered by the city's founding fathers in accommodating the flush toilet.

The problem began when Seattle's founding fathers chose to settle on a low peninsula that extended into a tidal mud flat. The nature of their poor choice wasn't known until the flush toilet found its way west in the 1880s. Like everybody else, Seattle's residents embraced the toilet with the same enthusiasm, it is said, that Californians now reserve for the hot tub. They also learned, in time, that effluents allowed to drain slowly, slowly into Puget Sound were very apt to return when the tide was high, with disconcerting results.

The residents responded with the ingenuity of the Seahawks adjusting their defense. They bolted their handsome porcelain toilets to the tops of elevated wooden thrones, so as to put distance between their bottoms and undesirable geysers. When one felt the urge, one climbed a short ladder. The newspapers helped out by publishing tables of the offending tides.

Eventually it was clear that this couldn't continue. Seattle had become a boom town, thanks to loggers, miners, and hookers. The city fathers settled upon a curious solution to their dilemma. They built stone walls at the curbs of the streets, reaching to the second floors of the buildings. They filled the areas between the walls with garbage, dead horses—anything that would take up space—and paved them over. The result was elevated streets. The merchants then put steel beams from the second floors of their establishments to the curbs of the elevated streets. This was then bricked over, and they had elevated sidewalks to match the elevated streets.

The toilets were moved to the second floor—which was now the first floor and ground level of Seattle. The city had effectively been jacked up one level. The toilets flushed just fine.

The merchants saw no good reason to close down the original sidewalks and used the original ground floors of their buildings as subterranean establishments—in the process creating an underground city. There were sidewalks under sidewalks, shops under shops. By the turn of the century the underground metropolis had become the center of vice in its various forms, but it was eventually boarded up and forgotten. Rats took over the maze of forgotten corridors, rooms, sidewalks, and vaults that surrounded Pioneer Place Park.

Aboveground things were pretty much the way they had been before the arrival of the toilet. The test always was how to survive the weather. Gray skies are the norm in Seattle for almost nine months out of the year. The residents sometimes have to endure rain for weeks without a break—a cold mist that drifts lazily in from Puget Sound.

A consequence of all this, the shrinks say, is a high suicide rate, rather like that suffered by the solemn Swedes. It's a rare day in Seattle when you can go for a walk in the sun between October and June. If you're single you can stay home and let your brain dissolve in front of the tube, which is rather like injecting yourself with cancer. If you're a private investigator, you hope for an interesting case to keep you busy.

On the fourth day of Melinda Prettybird's

disappearance, I received prospects of a second, more tranquil, and better-paying case. This one came in the form of a packet from the fancy Hillendale's department store in New York.

I opened the Hillendale's envelope first, wondering just what manner of New York problem had found its way to Seattle. I certainly wasn't a potential customer. Had one of Hillendale's employees run off with the payroll? Was Mr. Hillendale's daughter missing? Was there a Mr. Hillendale around these days? I didn't know.

There was a Hillendale's Christmas catalog inside, and a letter from a man named Roger Swanberg:

Dear Mr. Denson,

As you may know, we at Hillendale's reserve space in our catalog every year for a select offering of gourmet cuisine. We offer caviar from the Caspian sea, truffles, whole goose foie gras, and smoked salmon—all from Petrossian's of Paris. Petrossian's smoked salmon is the moist, translucent variety from Norway—found on Manhattan's most discriminating tables. We have, however, received inquiries asking whether we might not also offer the distinctive variety smoked by Native Americans.

Hillendale's is now negotiating with SalPacInc, a company owned by a Quinault Indian in Washington State, for the pur-

chase of smoked salmon. However, owing
to botulism poisoning from canned salmon
in Alaska a few years ago, our insurance
holder, Rozak and Stone, New York, requires a modest investigation of the Sal-
PacInc facilities. Your name was recom-
mended to us by the Seattle Chamber of
Commerce.

We would like to hire you, Mr. Denson—at
your usual rates—to accompany our buyer,
Augustus Poorman, on a brief visit to the
cannery on the Quinault Indian Reservation. This is located on the Pacific Coast of
the Olympic Peninsula, as we understand
it. You would be required to write an
independent report for Rozak and Stone.
You might want to look at page thirty-one
of our catalog. If you are available for the
assignment, please phone us soonest. Mr.
Poorman will return your call for an
appointment.

Swanberg added a New York telephone number. I turned to the gourmet food page. There it
was, Item 92, and I had to admit that the
photograph showing the Norwegian smoked
salmon decked out on a silver platter made it
look tempting. The copy said the smoked salmon
aficionado could buy two-and-three-quarter
pounds for a mere seventy bucks, plus another
twenty-five for the special delivery fee. This
was to insure freshness. That made me smile,
but I had to admit the salmon was cheaper

than their one-kilo tin of Beluga caviar at seven hundred bucks plus the twenty-five-dollar special delivery fee. I also had to snicker at the blurb's boast that the salmon were "line-caught." That was ridiculous. There was no difference between a salmon caught on a line and a salmon caught in a net.

I couldn't imagine any reason why I shouldn't lend a hand to the good folks at Hillendale's and check out the fish—it seemed like honest enough work. What did I care if they made a few thousand percent profit? At my usual rates? No haggling? Well, I didn't see why I shouldn't cash in too. I called the New York number.

"Doris Baldwin," a woman answered.

"My name is John Denson, I'm a private investigator in Seattle, Washington. I've received a letter from a Roger Swanberg. Do you have a Roger Swanberg in your firm?"

The woman laughed. "Yes, sir, we do, but I'm not sure you want to be talking to me."

"Would you please tell Mr. Swanberg that his Augustus Poorman should call me at his convenience?"

"Well, I guess I could," Ms. Baldwin said.

She sounded like she'd never heard of Poorman. "Why is it that I shouldn't be talking to you?" I asked.

"I work in public relations. Our buyers work in another department."

That was strange. I looked at my letter again. Swanberg's secretary had fouled up. The long-distance call was costing me money. "You'll get word to Mr. Swanberg? No problem or anything?"

"Sure," she said. "I'll give him the message."

9 SIRENS

We were well into a doubles match with a pair of elderly hippies from Sedro Wooley when the sirens began to wail. Willie was on the line facing a sixty-two; sirens outside the Doie were bothersome to Willie because of the warriors sitting in the shelter of the pergola across the street. Melinda Prettybird had now been missing four days.

"I hope one of those guys out there hasn't fucked-up," he said. "I don't need that on top of everything else." Willie gave the triple-ten a good stare. He moved his elbow under his hand and leaned forward just a tad.

I shut up so he could concentrate on his darts.

Willie turned his head. Another siren. A solo. Willie Prettybird hit a single ten, leaving him fifty-two. He scrunched his face and considered the board.

"Go for a fat twenty," I said. "If it comes to me, I'd rather face a thirty-two." If Willie shot a twelve, he'd have an out dart—a forty or a thirty-six—even if he hit the trip. If he shot for a twenty to leave a thirty-two, he risked bust-

66

ing on the trip. I liked the thirty-two, a sweet double-sixteen.

Willie didn't bust. He hit his single twenty and followed it with a clean double-sixteen to win the game and earn us a pitcher of Oly. Our opponents had to take a load of furniture to Tacoma in a U-Haul, so we had a chance to talk. Since the police had Mike Stark covered with a twenty-four-hour surveillance, we decided to concentrate on the possibility that Melinda's disappearance had to do with the Cowlitz fishing lawsuit.

I started to say something, then stopped. The sirens had returned.

Willie couldn't ignore the sirens anymore. He walked to the window to see what the fuss was about. He motioned for me to join him. I did, accompanied by Juantar Chauvin and the whole crowd at the Doie. "Praise Jesus!" Juantar said. "What's going on?"

Across the street Pioneer Place Park was swarming with Seattle policemen. Ten or twelve squad cars surrounded the park, blue lights flashing. Nobody had to be told this was heavy-duty action.

Willie Prettybird ran outside and tried to get across the street, but it was impossible. He returned, shaken, unable to take his eyes off the pergola.

"It'll be on the tube, Willie," I said. "All truth that matters appears on television, you know that."

"Poor bastards," he said.

"There's nothing you can do, Willie," I said.

There were probably just as many Indian dart throwers in Seattle as there were cowboys in Brooklyn; nevertheless Willie Prettybird was an ace. His stroke was lovely—all forearm, no body, the same every time. A fluid, smooth stroke. This skill in the hands of an Indian, of course, gave Juantar Chauvin an opportunity to exercise his overactive imagination.

Juantar wondered aloud if Willie's ancestors had not perfected that stroke throwing tomahawks at white men. "You should scalp somebody here in the Doie, Willie. We'd all like to see how it's done. We really would. Sure we would. Maybe you could use Denson's scalp. You wouldn't care, would you, Denson? A little baldness at the temple there, make you look distinguished."

"I think I'll pass, Juantar," I said.

"I got scalped by my mother's genes," he said. "Look't here." He leaned over and ran the palm of his hand over his balding forehead.

Juantar really got worked up a half-hour later when one of his customers said another hunk of human flesh had been found across the street. This one was frozen. Juantar paced the floor, giggling, making odd faces, acting goony, loose. "Praise Jesus, Willie, I was only kidding about the tomahawks. Really I was. You have to believe me." Juantar happily surveyed the Doie. "Everybody's all worked up. Look at 'em drink. Look at 'em. Makes 'em thirsty talking about all that blood." He swept his hand from one horizon of the Doie to the other in the manner of a rancher tracing the vista of his spread. "I love it," he said.

"You'd be fun to scalp, Juantar," Willie said.

Juantar ignored him. "A chunk of human flesh, waiting there for some dog to carry it off. Isn't it wonderful? At the bar they're saying the climate does it. Folks've got mildew on the brain."

Willie Prettybird wasn't as enthusiastic as Juantar. He looked at the pergola across the street.

Juantar said, "I thought you people just took scalps, Willie. I didn't hear anything about butchering people. Praise the Lord!"

Willie Prettybird was in no mood to joke. "Nobody mentioned the sex of that hunk of flesh they found across the street, did they?"

"Oh, come on, Willie," I said. The truth was, when a man's sister was threatened and then turns up missing, his mind works overtime. Willie Prettybird didn't like playing darts with his sister out there depending on him.

Willie sighed. "If Mike Stark isn't involved in this thing, then it probably has to do with this fishing mess, wouldn't you say?"

"There's a chance of it," I said.

"There's not a lot we can do about Stark without something concrete to go on." Willie folded his flights and tucked his darts away in a small leather folder.

"I didn't see anything. The cops haven't seen anything."

"Then maybe we should start looking into this salmon-fishing business just in case."

"That's what I'd do if it was my sister."

"I think you should talk to my lawyer, Janine Hallen. She really knows the ins and outs of this business. I can't talk about it without getting pissed off."

"Sure, I'll talk to Janine," I said.

"I'll call her in the morning. How about I have her drop by your place, ten o'clock, say. I swore I'd never blow my money on a lawyer unless I know for a fact he's one smart son of a bitch. If you want to have a good basketball team, you recruit blacks. If you want a smart lawyer, you get yourself someone Jewish."

"Is Hallen Jewish?"

"No," Willie said. "And she ain't even a he. But I bet you figured that out by her first name, didn't you, sleuth. She's a member of Mensa. Do you know what you have to have to be a member of Mensa?"

I thought I knew, but Willie would have been disappointed if he didn't get to tell me about it. "Never heard of it."

"You're going to go far in life, Denson, really far. A measured I.Q. above the ninety-eighth percentile, that's what you have to have. Janine Hallen doesn't have to bluff anybody when it comes to brains. Remember, ten o'clock. She's always on time. She has an orderly mind."

"No wallowing in the fart sack, I promise. I'll be caffeined up and ready to go."

10 SALMON

I can't say the alarm didn't go off because it did, with an infuriating *weeep! weeep! weeep!* programmed into it by some sadistic Japanese engineer. I reached over with the disdain of a karate master and whacked the damned thing silent. Who said I couldn't take something out if I wanted? I didn't feel like getting up; it was as warm as pond water at two o'clock under my electric blanket, when all of a sudden Winston began putting on a hell of an uproar outside my door.

Winston was a stuffed English pit bull who would continue to bark until his tape ran out or I answered the door. Winston had five taped barks of varying degrees of outlandishness that I changed whenever I got bored with a particular growl; I'd taped his current warning from a Doberman attack dog in the Army kennels at Fort Lewis. Lucifer's pooch or Satan's doggie could not have sounded meaner.

I grinned like a hog at supper, wondering who was at the door, and pulled on my yellow boxer shorts with the smoking six-shooter printed on the front.

Outside, from a speaker above the door, a proper English friend of mine was saying, beneath Winston's uproar: "Please check your nose for visible boogers. Master Denson will be with you shortly."

I remembered my appointment with Willie Prettybird's lawyer when I opened the door and saw a woman standing there with a briefcase in her hand. She was wearing a proper blue skirt and one of those imitation men's jackets worn by professional women and subscribers to *Cosmo*. She was a natural blond, a trifle shy, with pale blue eyes. She looked a bit like the actress Barbara Eden, who once played a genie on a television program. When I was a kid, I used to groan over the very mention of Barbara Eden.

The blond lady said, "Mr. Denson?"

"Yes, ma'am," I said.

"You should shampoo your dog, Mr. Denson; it would make his coat shine. My name is Janine Hallen, Willie Prettybird's attorney." She either had good peripheral vision or great self-control, because she appeared not to notice the six-shooter on my underwear.

"I'd like to take Winston for a walk, but he's too heavy to carry," I said. "Did Willie tell you about him?"

"I'd been warned."

"Well, won't you come in," I said, and pulled on a pair of jeans.

Janine Hallen ignored me as I dressed. She walked around the walls examining the memorabilia I had taped, nailed, and tied to the walls—a poster here, a photo of a laughing woman there, pennants of Dutch and Spanish soccer teams.

"I've been told you're an accomplished detective, Mr. Denson."

"Hell, nobody better," I said. "Sleuth is my first name."

"A good detective, they say, but quirky."

"Depends on what you think is normal." I zipped my fly with a flourish; I was dressed.

Janine remained cool. "That's true," she said. She was analytical, careful. She regarded me with interest, as though I were a curious but harmless lunatic.

"Orderly room, tight mind," I said. I gestured for her to sit in my chair. I took the love seat. "I suppose Willie told you our problem. Melinda's been gone for five days now. The cops are watching Mike Stark, so there's not much we can do except wait . . ."

". . . or see if Melinda's disappearance has anything to do with the Cowlitz salmon lawsuit."

"Exactly," I said.

"Could it have anything to do with Moby Rappaport?"

"Anything's possible, I guess."

Janine Hallen put a trim fingernail on her lower lip. "If something's happened to Moby Rappaport we'll draw Awdrey—did Willie tell you that?"

"No, he didn't," I lied. "Who's Awdrey? Do I

call you Ms. Hallen? Janine? What? Willie said you were a Mensa and I'm kind of scared."

She knew how to laugh, which was reassuring. "Call me Janine. Judge Louise Awdrey hates Indians, did Willie tell you that?"

"He said lawyers call her John Wayne because she likes to blow Indians off their ponies."

Hallen turned her knees a little more away from my angle. "If we draw Awdrey I'll have to start from scratch. Maybe you'll find them both, Melinda and Rappaport."

"That's possible. To ask the right questions, I have to learn a little more about this salmon quarrel. I learned some from Mike Stark the other day, but Willie says I should talk to you."

"The sport fishermen and the commercial fishermen have both filed briefs as friends of the court—that'd be Foxx Jensen and Doug Egan. You should probably start with them."

"I have to know motives. What they stand to gain or lose in this lawsuit, for example."

Janine Hallen adjusted her jacket. "Salmon are what's called a 'common good,' Mr. Denson— a resource available to everybody. This case all boils down to who gets how much of the fish. Salmon spawn in fresh water, swim out to the ocean, and come back as adults to spawn again. Part of the time they're in international waters, subject to Japanese or Canadian or Russian fishermen, and so out of our control."

"The courts divvy the catch," I said.

"Yes, they do. Dividing a fish run is harder than allocating timber harvests. If you catch too many fish this year, there'll be fewer next year. The state regulates the catch so that the runs aren't destroyed. The Indians have always understood that they had to let some of the fish pass one year so they'd have something to catch the next."

"Clever Redskins."

"The closer to the rivers you get, the larger the salmon are; they're concentrated in the rivers. At sea they're scattered, small, and expensive to find."

"What happened to Willie's ancestors?"

"Some of the Indians swapped their timber for the right to catch half the fish at the rivers where they fished. Most of the tribes signed agreements with the state of Washington in 1854 and 1855. These were Washington rivers. Unfortunately, the Cowlitz, the Wahkiakum, and the Chinook fished tributaries of the Columbia."

"The lower Columbia being the border between Oregon and Washington."

"That's right, making it a federal dispute. The Columbia tribes signed treaties with the government, but Congress never got around to ratifying them. Not that the treaty tribes did much better. In 1914, non-Indian fishermen started stretching seine nets in front of the Indian fish traps."

"Oops."

"Yes. Then came the gillnets. They're not as good as seine nets, but they can be used farther out to sea."

"Smaller fish."

"That wasn't the end of it. The trollers were willing to accept even immature fish to beat the gillnets. Not only that, but the runs were being depleted by hydroelectric dams and industrial pollution that the state made no effort to control. Then in 1974 a federal judge named George Boldt said the Indians were in fact entitled to half the salmon entering their accustomed fishing places—just like it said in their treaties with the state of Washington."

"Oh, boy!"

"He said the state had to restore the salmon runs and to see to it that the treaty Indians got their fish."

"Good for them," I said.

"The only problem was that commercial fishermen went about business as usual."

"They ignored the decision?"

"Yep. But the Supreme Court upheld Boldt in 1979. The treaty Indians get half, plus an amount for subsistence and ceremonial purposes. If the Indians eat a fish at home, they have to fill out a card and turn it in to the state."

"Have they run over their fifty percent share?"

"In the first years after Boldt they were running about ten percent; lately that's gone up to about thirty percent. The people at the Washington State Fish and Wildlife Commission have to watch this carefully; they're getting better at it because every side has its own biologists. If non-Indians stray too far over their allotted share, Indian lawyers will take them to court. It's tough, Mr. Denson. State biologists have to make decisions very quickly, often based on insufficient data. If they grant too much time, they risk harming the run. If they're too restrictive they hurt the fishing industry, and the price to the consumer rises. All of this, Mr. Denson, ignores the foreign fishermen—Japanese, Canadians, and Soviets— who fish international waters. Salmon runs crisscross at sea. They're hard to follow, much less monitor."

"Listen, I'd like some coffee," I said. "Do you mind if I make a pot of coffee while we talk?"

"If you include legal fees and the cost of boosting the runs with hatchery fish, each fish can cost Washington State two or three hundred dollars. Depends on who you talk to. Raising hatchery fish isn't easy. In 1981 a Weyerhauser ocean ranching firm managed to release 2.8 million fingerlings that were blind."

"What?"

"A company in Oregon hatched a batch that turned right at the Columbia instead of left, went upstream instead of down." Hallen smiled at the kicker of her anecdote.

I said, "What happened to the commercial fishermen whose take was reduced?"

"Congress was pressured into appropriating $3.4 million to buy licensed boats from fishermen facing bankruptcy. The idea was to reduce the size of the commercial fleet so those left could earn a decent living."

I dumped some generic coffee into the filter of my machine. "How did that work out?"

"A licensed salmon boat wasn't worth much after Boldt, but prices rose when there was federal money in the pot. Some fishermen sold a few of their boats at inflated prices and used the profit to buy more efficient gear for the rest of their fleet. Others went to Alaska, where there were no treaty Indians. The commercial fishermen say they're being pushed out of business. The trouble is their statistics are muddied by part-timers and school teachers who fish in the summer and claim tax losses to pay for a boat that's recreational the rest of the year."

"What about the sport fishermen?" I poured us both a cup of coffee.

"The sport fishermen are the most powerful today. There are more of them, and many of them are in positions of power in both government and private industry. They get a lot of attention in the newspapers and on television. The sport fishermen are the least efficient, which the state likes. The fact is they're so inefficient that if we banned commercial fishing there could be too many salmon for the rivers."

I said, "Heavens, we wouldn't want that."

"The gillnetters and seiners get their income from chums, pinks, and sockeye, but the hatcheries have to breed chinook and coho, the only varieties that will hit an artificial lure. Sports licensing doesn't come close to paying for state-hatched fish—the taxpayer springs for that."

"Sure, subsidize them. Why not? Some people turn a little loony at the thought of high bucks. Do Foxx Jensen and Doug Egan strike you as the kind of people who would do violence to Melinda Prettybird to have their way in this mess? I want to know what you think, gut feelings, no hedges."

Janine Hallen took a sip of coffee before she got down to the nitty-gritty. She leaned forward, considering. She was a lawyer. She was a judicious, careful woman. She said, "If the circumstances were right, I think either one of those two would be capable of harming Melinda Prettybird."

11 LIARS AND LISTENING DEVICES

It turned out that nobody had harmed Melinda Prettybird—yet—not Mike Stark, not Foxx Jensen, not Doug Egan. Willie and I were ready to drive to Scappoose the next morning, when Melinda called him at the Doie. Willie talked to her on Juantar's telephone, mouthing "Melinda" to me as he listened to her story. His face turned from surprise, to anger, to bewilderment, to disgust, roughly in that order.

"Women!" he said, when he had finished.

"Is she okay?"

"She's fine, except now the guy says he's gonna kill her."

"What?"

"She got a note in the mail."

"What happened?"

"You want it from the beginning?"

"Might as well," I said.

"Melinda says she had the feeling she was being watched after I called her the other night. She thought she might be in danger and didn't want to wait there by herself, so she left me a note and took off to see her friend in

80

Scappoose. She says she stopped twice to call me on her way to Oregon—once at Olympia, once at Chehalis."

"But you were spending our last night at the Pig's."

"Next to the last, I think. When she got to Scappoose she and her friend thought it would be safest to go someplace where they couldn't be traced. They decided to go to the Oregon coast for a couple of days to hunt blue agates on the beach. On their way to Seaside they stopped off at Rodney's in Astoria to call me. No answer. Rodney says no problem, he'll let me know she's okay."

"Only brother Rodney doesn't bother."

"The asshole!" Little brother was going to be in for it when Willie caught up with him.

"So what did the note say?"

"The guy says he's killed once, she's next. She tried the Pig's first, and when it was closed, she called your answering service."

"Does she know where Rodney is?"

"No. And she's scared to death. She wants to go back to Scappoose. I told her we want to talk to her first. She says to hurry. She's got Prib there for protection, but she wants to get going."

"Prib?"

"Remember me mentioning my bricklayer friend, Prib Ostrow? Rodney and I grew up with him down in Mossyrock. We were insepa-rable. Hell, one time . . ." Willie shook his head at the memory ". . . we even made him a blood brother. You know what I mean—wrist to wrist stuff, mixing red man's blood with a white man's. We got the idea from watching an old Jeff Chandler movie. Anyway, Prib's up in Seattle for a few months on a job. Melinda is special to him. Prib'll want to help."

"Let's get going, then. I agree that she should hustle back to Scappoose . . ."

Willie was halfway to the door before I could finish the sentence.

When Willie opened the door to his sister's apartment, Melinda met him with a long, hard hug. "I'm sorry, Willie. You must have been worried sick. Rodney said he'd take care of letting you know we were okay. He said we should go, enjoy ourselves."

"Everything's okay now," Willie said.

"The kids just loved it down there, Willie. You should have seen them."

I don't think I'd ever seen a man disarmed as easily as Willie Prettybird. "It was nothing, sis. Really. What we have to do now is get on with running this guy down."

"Oh, thank you, Willie," she said.

Willie said, "But from now on you have to let me know where you are. No relying on Rodney—you know him. With a screwball running around threatening you, I have to know."

"I promise, Willie." A little boy with Melinda's look about his face tugged at her leg. She hoisted him up on her forearm.

A large-bellied man was sitting on an overstuffed sofa watching a television game show.

He took a swig out of a stubby of Rainier and rose as Melinda introduced him and her two small sons.

"This is Gary. This is Bert." Melinda bounced the child on her forearm by way of indicating he was Bert. "And that's Michael." She nodded toward a boy of two or three who peered from around the corner. Michael headed for his Uncle Willie.

The game-show host, a man named Richard, kissed a fat lady standing with her family. Gary said, "Jesus, they must pay that guy a lot of money. How'd you like to kiss something like that? So you're the detective Melinda an' Willie's been talkin' about. Willie's dart-throwing friend." He grinned. He was impressed. "The detective!" he said. He stood, shoulders back, surveying his stomach. He had the girth of Friar Tuck or Falstaff. He embraced Willie. "By God, you can count on me, Willie. We'll get the son of a bitch. No problem." He released Willie from his grip and said to me, "Willie 'n Rodney 'n me're blood brothers. Willie tell you that?"

"Sure did," I said.

"I may have a few pounds in the gut, but I can move if I have to. Ain't that right, Willie?"

"Prib used to be quick on his feet," Willie said.

Gary gave Willie a scornful look. "Whaddya mean, used to be quick?" Gary demonstrated his quickness by shifting rapidly from side to side on the balls of his feet like a prizefighter about to be introduced. "Listen, I want you to call me Prib like Willie does. A friend of his is a friend of mine." Prib turned off the game show with Richard the host in the middle of kissing another matronly lady. Prib extended his hand.

"Prib it is," I said. We pumped with much sincerity.

"Me'n Willie played football together in high school. Ain't that right, Willie?" Prib didn't wait for an answer. He turned his stomach toward Melinda. "Go ahead, sis." Melinda glanced at me and gave Prib a hard uppercut in the stomach. He looked at me, pleased. "Do it again!" She gave him a right cross the second time, swinging from her heels. "Again. Pretend I'm that little pervert fucker." Melinda unloaded on him a third time. I couldn't have taken a blow like that. "That ain't just flab," Prib said.

"Looks like a tank of Rainier to me." Willie winked at me and hoisted his nephew onto his shoulders.

"Shit, too," Prib said. "I got this gut settin' choke out of Centralia." Prib rammed his stomach against the top of the couch, sumo-style, and tipped it over, sending cushions flying. Little Bert and Michael watched in awe. Melinda and Willie were amused. Prib, having proven his point, set about putting the couch back together.

"You big fart," Melinda said.

"I'd like to work with you'n Willie to flush

that little pinch of shit out of his hole," Prib said.

"This kind of thing usually requires a lot of legwork. Pretty boring," I said.

Prib grabbed my hand again and squeezed hard. "I'll do what has to be done," he murmured. "Mike Stark! I seen that guy."

Melinda took little Bert and Michael to bed so they wouldn't hear any more truth than they already knew about their father. Prib opened bottles of Rainier for everybody, and we settled around the formica top of the kitchen table to figure out how to track our man. Melinda gave us the note she had received and we considered it over our Rainiers. It was handwritten in block letters, just like the one that had been handed to her the night her last boyfriend was beaten. This message was a bit more pointed than the first one:

I HAVE KILLED ONCE. YOU'RE NEXT.

"Whoa!" Willie said. Melinda had told him about the note on the phone, but seeing it was somehow more shocking.

"So what did he look like, Melinda?" I said.

Melinda put her small hands flat on the table, palms down. "He's maybe five nine or ten, something like that. Medium build, I guess. I can't say much beyond that. He always wears a ski mask over his head, so I can't see his face. He wears gloves, so I can't see his hands."

"Mike Stark's size?"

"Yes, roughly. All of a sudden he's there in my bedroom assaulting whoever's with me. At first I thought it was a nut, but now I think it's Mike or someone working for him. He has to be behind it, has to be. He said he'd never let another man have me, never. All kinds of people heard him threaten me, all kinds. What I can't understand is why the cops don't do something about him?"

"The police have got him under surveillance. They can't do anything until they have some proof."

"If he's got money enough to hire a thug," Willie said, "he's got enough money to buy an alibi."

Melinda said, "He sits up there at the university, a big-deal professor living off his family's money. I've got two kids to take care of by myself. Two kids and he won't let me have another man. A scholar. Hah!" Melinda's face tightened.

"Let me ask you this," I said. "How is it, do you suppose, that Mike knows you're going to spend a night with a man? I mean, how is it that he even knows when you have a boyfriend?"

"I don't know, John, I just don't know. He knows. He just knows. It's like he's following me or something—it's spooky. Mike Stark's got enough money, he probably does have somebody following me."

"He doesn't want you, but he doesn't want anyone else to either."

"That's precisely it," she said. "Big-deal professor. Big-deal friend of the Indians." She looked scornful. "He has everybody fooled—even Willie. Such a nice guy, they think. They should see what he's doing to me."

Willie said, "The son of a bitch."

"Just let me get ahold of him," Prib muttered. He was furious. The latent sumo in him took over again; he gave the table a nudge with his stomach.

"If you two are going to work with me, Prib, it'll have to be the safe way. We just want to find the guy; we'll let the cops do the rest. We're not some kind of posse like in the movies. We have to leave open the possibility it might not be Mike."

Prib was unconvinced. "Professors," he said. He spared the table and bumped an imaginary opponent with his sumo stomach.

"Melinda, is there anything at all about the assailant that might help us out—assuming it might not be Mike Stark. And what about Mike? What does Mike do? Does he have any hobbies? What does he do on weekends?"

"Mostly he sits around and reads. Once in a while he gets adventurous and looks for mushrooms. His idea of a party is to stand around and talk about where he found his last stupid batch of mushrooms and drink the cheapest red wine that has a cork. God, the music he used to play. What a bore. If I ever have to listen to 'Take Five' again, I think I'll kill myself." Her eyes told me she thought I probably listened to more interesting music.

I could have told her I liked accordions, and her eyes would still have danced. "Professors are full of fertilizer, Melinda, that's their profession. They're all that way. If you're a punker you dye your hair green to shock people. If you're a professor you listen to scratchy old Brubeck records to impress everyone. What I want to know is, what does he do that other professors don't ordinarily do?"

"Well, I don't know, other than the mushrooms. He even got Willie and Rodney interested in them." She looked at Willie, who grinned foolishly. "That and he drives a restored 1939 Ford coupe that he polishes every Saturday."

"Nothing else?"

"No."

"Do you mind if I take a look at your phone?"

"Look wherever you want," Melinda said.

There was a gadget screwed onto the underside of the end table that held Melinda's telephone.

Melinda stared. Willie and Prib leaned over the table, grinning at the gadget. "What's it do?" Willie asked.

"It's a bug. It records whatever is said in this room and relays it to a voice-activated recorder stashed away in this building somewhere." I saw there was an engraving on the back of the recorder: SPD.

"Seattle Police Department?" Willie asked.

"I'd bet on it," I said. "Did the cops ever say they wanted to tap your phone?"

Melinda looked surprised. "Don't they have to get a court order to use those things without asking you?"

"Good question. Last time I knew, they had to get a court order," I said. "I suppose I better ask the cops about the damned thing." I gave each of them one of my business cards. "This number is the Puget Sound Answering Service. Any one of you can leave a message for me. The sexy-voiced one is Emma; she handles most of my calls. The strange-voiced one is Virginia. The young man is Clyde. If Virginia or Clyde handle your call, make sure you have everything clear."

Melinda Prettybird put her hand on mine. "There's one thing you must remember about Mike Stark, John. You must remember. He'll come across as generous and civilized, a little quirky perhaps, but then again he's a professor. He'll charm you and win you over and lie all the while. You mustn't be fooled. You mustn't. Sometimes I wonder if he's forgotten what the truth really is. It's like he lives in two worlds. I think he's nuts, I really do."

"A liar," I said.

Melinda said, "A liar like you just wouldn't believe."

12 DETECTIVE WILLIS

I listened to the radio as I drove to the police station the next morning: a frozen human chop had been found behind the pergola in Pioneer Place Park. I punched several buttons on my radio; the newscasters all led with the same story—that's because most of them used nearly identical news roundups written by the Associated Press or UPI. I don't think any of the newscasters had bothered to edit the story. The coroner, on tape, said a "sharp instrument" had been used to cut the object from the calf of a human corpse. The coroner identified the victim as a Caucasian male, possibly the body that had yielded the frozen steak a day earlier.

I was glad to hear the killer was smart enough not to try cutting a frozen corpse with a dull instrument. The terms "chop" and "steak" were added by the wire service reporter in the interest of freaking people out on a slow news day.

Folks in Seattle were secretly thrilled over a butchered human showing up on First Avenue. They were sensitive to their town's image; they longed for the status and trappings of a Big-Time City. Big-Time Cities have at least two things in common: big-league franchises in all sports and a crime story bizarre enough to make both the newsmagazines and the network news. Seattle had the Mariners, the Seahawks, and the Super-Sonics, but couldn't match Boston's strangler, San Francisco's zodiac killer, Los Angeles's hillside strangler, or Atlanta's killer of young boys. Police reporters in New York were said to get bored with such yawners as a quadruple murder and suicide in Harlem or a family of nine getting torched in the Bronx. It is a curious country in which the residents of a city feel inferior because their city is relatively safe to live in.

The Seattle police would just as soon pass on butchered human bodies, thanks. The sergeant at the desk was listening to the latest on a transistor radio when I brought in the SPD listening device. His badge said he was M. Gilman. I slid the bug out of a paper bag onto the desk like it was some kind of rare scientific specimen.

M. Gilman raised an eyebrow. He looked at me. He made a clicking sound with his tongue, like I was a naughty boy. He leaned over and looked at the gadget without touching it. He whistled. He looked up at me. "You do know what this is, I take it." He whistled the opening bars of Beethoven's Fifth.

"Oh, yes, I know what it is." I leaned over and peered at it close up.

Gilman whistled more Beethoven. "You want to tell me where you got it?"

"Found it in a lady's house. It says SPD there and has a number."

"We put those things out there for a reason, you know."

"Nobody asked the lady for her okay. We were sort of wondering."

Gilman ran his hand over his face. "Well, maybe she's being investigated for some reason, did you ever stop to think of that? We may be dumb cops, but we don't go around saying, 'Hey, lady! Okay if we can bug your house so we can throw you in jail?' "

"I don't think she's under suspicion of anything," I said.

"And you are?"

"John Denson." I showed him my private investigator's I.D.

He examined the license, turned on his swivel chair, and punched some numbers into a computer keyboard. He watched as my police dossier appeared on the screen in neat green letters. Gilman scrolled it with keys on the console and we both read.

"I was really born in Weiser," I said. "The certificate was registered in Boise, that's all."

"Never had it changed, huh?"

"Couldn't see the point in it."

Gilman studied the dossier, then punched a number on his phone. "Donna, this is Max Gilman. Can you tell me if we have a court order for a clandestine listening device?" He gave her the number engraved on the instrument. "I see," he said. "Can you tell me where it was supposed to be?" He listened, watching me. "Thank you, Donna. What was the address where you found this, Mr. Denson?"

I told him the address.

Gilman thought that over. "I guess we better see Willis." Gilman pushed the listening device back into the bag with his own pencil and rose, addressing a younger man who was working studiously at his own terminal. "Can you sit in for a few minutes, Larry, I gotta take this guy down to see Willis?"

Larry seemed surprised. "Willis?"

"I don't know what else to do?"

"You get paid to make decisions, I guess," Larry said.

"Are you going to give me a receipt for that?" I asked.

Gilman smiled. "Sure," he said. He slid the bug out so he could get the registration number. He took his time, I thought. When he finished he disappeared for a couple of minutes and returned with a couple of folders. One of them, I saw, had Melinda Prettybird's name on it.

I followed Gilman down a series of halls to a door marked LT. RICHARD WILLIS. There was a worn paperback volume of *Finnegans Wake* on his desk. He was a good-looking man, with silver hair and a small, neat mustache. He wore a three-piece checked suit, with a neat bow tie. He had one of those rare expressive faces that moved fluidly from interest to scorn and disdain.

Gilman slid the listening device onto Willis's desk. "You might want to check the number on your list."

Without introducing himself to me, Willis looked at the serial number on the listening device, then retrieved a ledger from a small safe. He checked the number against a list. He gave me a look that was not kind; he was not immediately attracted to people who came in dragging listening devices that belonged to the Seattle police. "Where'd you get this?"

I gave him Melinda Prettybird's name and address.

Willis pursed his lips.

"Ms. Prettybird was wondering why she was being bugged," I said.

Gilman laughed from behind me. He handed Willis a folder.

Willis read the file carefully. "And you are?"

"John Denson. I'm a private investigator."

Willis looked at Gilman, then furrowed his eyebrows. "You check his bona fides?" Willis asked.

"He's as okay as these guys get," Gilman said. He handed Willis a second folder.

Willis opened the second folder and glanced at the contents. "I want to know when you found it."

"Last night, screwed onto the bottom of the lady's end table."

"Hmmmm," Willis said.

"Some guy's been threatening her."

Willis looked at the first folder again. "We got people working on that?"

"Following her ex-husband?"

"Yes."

"I heard the guys talking about it," Gilman said. He looked impassive and whistled *wh-wh-wh-whooo*. More Beethoven. "Ex-husband's a loony."

"The bug have to do with Melinda or the guy who has been beating up her boyfriends?" I asked.

Willis pretended I hadn't asked the question. "We know how to get in touch with Denson here?" he asked Gilman.

Gilman said, "I'll make sure his stuff's up-to-date before I let him go."

"Thanks for bringing this back to us, Mr. Denson," Willis said. "Concerned citizens like you save the taxpayer a lot of money." He made it clear I was one concerned citizen he could do without.

"The lady's going to want some kind of explanation of how that thing came to be in her apartment," I said.

Willis sighed. "Or what, Mr. Denson? Just what the hell are you going to do? For all you know she's some kind of felon."

"Or I'll have to take it to internal investigations, call the newspapers and all that," I said.

Willis looked at Max Gilman.

Gilman said, "His poop sheet says he's a

former newspaper reporter. He asked for a receipt. Not much I could do."

Willis looked sour. His range of expressions was impressive. "We got a federal fucking judge missing. We got pieces of a human body showing up at Pioneer Place Park. I have to sit on my ass waiting for a goddamn hearing. I figure what the hell, maybe I'll get a little reading in." He nudged the paperback on his desk. "Now this. You'll excuse my temper, I'm sure, Mr. Private Investigator."

"Maybe the parts'll turn out to be the judge," I said. "Did you ever think about that? It'd simplify the investigation. Save us all a lot of money."

"I'm sure somebody around here has considered that possibility, Mr. Denson. They may be slow, but they do their best. I know you're not required to tell me what you're working on, Mr. Denson, but if it has to do with Ms. Prettybird's boyfriends, that involves assault and battery. If whatever you're doing has to do with Judge Moby Rappaport, you're looking at possible kidnaping and murder. That, too, is our business. If you hear anything regarding any of that then you come running quick, quick." Willis snapped his fingers with a *pop! pop!* that startled me.

"Maybe I'll run onto something you can use. You can probably always use the help."

Richard Willis gave me a patient look. Then he turned his head at a slight angle and looked uncomprehending. "Help? Mr. Denson, the silly fuckers around here don't need help—what are you talking about?" He adjusted his bow tie again, as if to recompose himself. He said, "Will you get this asshole out of here, Gilman."

I started to leave with Gilman, but Willis stood and motioned with his hand for me to stop. "I remember your name now, you're the P.I. who used to be a friend of Captain Gilberto aren't you?" Willis obviously trusted Gilberto.

"He was a good cop," I said. Gilberto was now police chief in a small town in Northern California.

"You do get anything on this, you *will* give me a call, won't you, Mr. Denson?" Willis was enraged at something, but I didn't think it was me. He looked at Gilman as if to ask, well, Sergeant, how did I do? "Remember, Lieutenant Willis," he said to me.

Lieutenant Willis was in some kind of trouble. I wondered what it was. "Thanks much, Lieutenant," I said. "You *will* find out about that bug for me won't you?"

Richard Willis grimaced and said, "Check back in a couple of days."

He didn't look like he wanted to say a whole lot more, so I shut up.

13 HILLENDALE'S CALLING

When I got back from my visit with M. Gilman and Richard Willis, I checked in with the Puget Sound Answering Service and Emma, of the wonderful voice. Virginia, the strange-voiced one, answered, and transferred me to Emma. I could hear Clyde, the excited one, saying, "It's Denson, it's Denson," in the background.

"Mr. Denson?" Emma said.

Emma's voice made me want to groan. Her voice was rich like the actress Suzanne Pleshette's; it breathed like the singer Karen Carpenter's used to. "Emma, my new clients are Willie and Rodney Prettybird, and their sister, Melinda. They'll be leaving messages for me."

Emma hesitated. She'd been reading the papers. "Prettybird?"

"They're Cowlitz, Emma."

"Does this have anything to do with that missing judge, Mr. Denson?"

"Nothing to do with that, Emma."

I could hear Clyde saying, "Somebody's been chopping the judge up. You wait. Ask Denson what he thinks, Emma, go ahead."

I said, "And you might also get a call from a

woman named Janine Hallen—she's the lawyer for the Prettybirds."

"A woman lawyer, Mr. Denson?"

"She sure looks like it to me. Yes, she does."

"You've talked to her, then. Mr. Denson, you know from experience you should ask my advice when you meet a lady, and feel ..." she lowered her voice, "... you know what I mean."

"Who says there's any you-know-what-I-means involved here?"

"Poontang! Poontang!" Clyde laughed. He was a reader and knew his American slang, however dated.

Emma said, "Clyde!" Then, "I know you, Mr. Denson. I've handled your calls for three years now. This woman operates from the left hemisphere, I'll bet, analytical, reserved, orderly. A firstborn probably, defender of the faith."

"All those things," I said.

"You freak those kind of ladies out, Mr. Denson. Leave them to men who wear neckties and have their cars washed. Clyde went out to the Doie, you know, we were all curious. He said the man who owned the bar gave some kind of mock evangelical sermon to the people at the bar."

Clyde yelled, "He said if we all drank a pitcher of Henry Weinhard's we'd be forgiven our sins."

Emma said, "You're a Doie kind of man, you know that, Mr. Denson."

I knew that. All we right-hemisphere youngest sons keep hoping we can find a woman who appreciates the Bohemian in us. "Did Clyde save himself?" I asked.

"Please don't humor him, Mr. Denson. He gets terrible headaches when he drinks too much."

"How about calls?"

"You got one long-distance from New York. Says his name's Augustus Poorman, a buyer from Hillendale's. Are you going to work for Hillendale's, Mr. Denson?"

"Well, I don't know . . ."

"My cousin went to Hillendale's on her trip to New York. Mr. Poorman declined to leave a message, by the way. He said he'd call again shortly."

No sooner had I hung up when Augustus Poorman did just that. He sounded like a frog in a barrel on the long-distance telephone connection; his voice was deep, resonant, assured. He was also Southern by origin, as Juantar was, but Texas-Southern, not Louisiana. "This is Augustus Poorman of Hillendale's, here in New York. I'd like to speak to Mr. John Denson, please, the private investigator."

"That's me," I said.

"Did y'all get our note and the catalog, Mr. Denson?"

"I sure did, Mr. Poorman. I have to tell you, though, I thought your caviar was a bit pricey at seven hundred bucks a can."

Poorman laughed. With a voice like that, he could have had a career in politics. "Y'all do check out, Mr. Denson. The Better Business Bureau, the Seattle Police Department, the County Prosecutor's Office. One of your former clients gave us a recommendation. A straight-forward investigator, he says. No *caca de toro*."

"I do my best."

"Hillendale's may be New York, you know, but I want you to know you're dealing with a Texan. I used to be a buyer for Neiman-Marcus down there in Dallas before one of them New York headhunters gave me a call. They wanted a Texan who knew quality, Mr. Denson. If a man's a real Texan, his word means something. My great-great-grandaddy went down at the Alamo. Stood right in there with Sam Houston and old Jim Bowie. If Hillendale's wanted to market barbecued penguin, Mr. Denson, I'd get 'em young King, fresh out of the Weddell Sea and all slathered down with brown sugar and vinegar and tomato sauce and cooked over hickory smoke, nothing but. What do you know about smoked salmon, Mr. Denson?"

"I buy it at the Pike Place Market all the time. Expensive."

"The people here at Hillendale's tell me they want salmon that's been smoked by Indians in a traditional Indian manner. Probably pressure from liberals, there're plenty of those in New York—all those Jews and all. You know what I mean, Denson. They want the best. That's what they pay me to buy. That's what I'm gonna buy. By God, that's a Texan's way of doing business. Ain't that right?"

"Oh, hell, yes. I think an outfit on the Quinault Indian Reservation smokes some qual-ity fish. I'm not sure who else."

"Why, those are our people. SalPacInc, it's called. I've got an appointment to take a look at their setup on Tuesday. Yes, SalPacInc. I want to make sure Hillendale's gets what it pays for."

That seemed easy enough. "I don't know why not," I said.

"We'll eat a little smoked fish and drink whatever it is they drink up there in the Pacific Northwest."

I checked my little notebook. "Tuesday looks good by me. It'll cost you three hundred bucks a day and expenses."

"You pay people right and you can expect good work. I pay first-class prices for first-class service. Say, how would it be if my secretary leaves word with your answering service so you can meet me at the airport? She can leave the flight number and all. Would that be a big bother, Mr. Denson?"

"No bother at all. That'd be Sea-Tac. See you Tuesday," I said. With all his y'alls and all, Augustus Poorman didn't sound very New York and Hillendale's, but that was okay; I tried not to be prejudiced against Texans or anybody else until I caught them crapping in my oatmeal.

I cracked a can of Oly, kicked back in my chair, and turned on the radio to see if there was any new outrage being reported from Pioneer Place Park. There was. Another human steak was found in the grass there—just behind the pergola bench.

14 MAN IN A WHITE HAT

Augustus Poorman's secretary gave Emma the flight number and the time of her boss's arrival at Sea-Tac Airport, but not a whole lot more. I didn't know what he looked like. I got my corduroy jacket cleaned for the occasion—although I thought a necktie was a bit much—and was at the correct arrival gate at the appointed hour to meet the Hillendale's buyer. I waited, somewhat nervously, as the passengers disgorged from the Boeing 747. What would a man like Poorman wear?

Then a tiny little man stepped through the door, and I knew I had my man. For some reason he looked like he had a big voice. He wore an elegant suit of tailored British wool and a white, high-peaked cowboy hat, like Tom Mix wore in the movies and Dan Blocker in the *Bonanza* television series. And gloves. He wore neat little black gloves, an affectation that somehow enhanced the cowboy hat. He glanced about the waiting area, looked at me, grinned, and walked my way, hand extended.

"Name's Augustus Poorman. Y'all'd be John Denson, I'm bettin'."

"That's my handle," I said.

Poorman laughed. "Y'all had the look of a man waiting for someone he hadn't seen before. I shoulda said something to my gal."

"You'd make a pretty fair detective yourself, Mr. Poorman. I do like that hat." The gloves, too, I might have added. He was either a fraud or the genuine article cast against type by a cunning Hillendale's management. I didn't see how he could be much in the middle.

"Folks got a right to expect a little extra when they're dealing with a Texan, Mr. Denson; I learned that when I bought for Neiman-Marcus. A weasel-mouth can't wear a hat like this and get away with it, if y'all know what I mean."

I'd seen all kinds of weasel-mouths in my time, but I let that one pass. "Pleased to meet you. I've got my Fiat gassed, and we've got people waiting to see us at the Quinault Indian Reservation. It's a bit of a drive. We have to go south through Tacoma to Olympia at the southern end of the Sound, and from there to the coast."

"Don't mind a little drivin', I grew up in West Texas. Thought nothing of drivin' a hundred miles to do a little honky-tonkin'." He pronounced Texas Tex-is. That sounded genuine.

We retrieved Poorman's luggage and in a half-hour were on our way south, moving through a light rain. Poorman seemed to enjoy the ride and was full of questions as he read road signs.

"Y'all've got some mighty pretty country up here, Mr. Denson, but with all this rain, I'd be afraid of having my joints rust."

"You're probably better off in Arizona if you have arthritis," I said.

We got to the Quinault Reservation a little more than an hour later, and I pulled up at the information center. A pregnant girl with pretty brown eyes gave us a map of the reservation. She used a stubby pencil to trace the route to the SalPacInc smokehouse. "Mr. Davis is expecting you, Mr. Denson," she said. She could hardly keep her eyes off Augustus Poorman and his hat. "I hope you like our salmon," she said. "They say it's the best in the world."

"I'm sure I'll like it a lot," Poorman said. When we got into the Fiat, he said, "Advertising people are pretty damned good at writing fiction, Mr. Denson. Y'all'd just be amazed at what people will feed you and call good food. Sometime when you've got an empty stomach, y'all should ask me about the chocolate mousse I sampled down in Dallas one time. Folks had the gall to think they were gonna sell that stuff to a Neiman-Marcus buyer. Hell, I had refried beans in Nacogdoches once that tasted a damn sight better, if you know what I mean."

I said, "The way I hear it, a Texan'll try to sell you anything."

Poorman laughed heartily. "Hell, son, all Texans're full of manure, we both know that. When I got hooked up with Hillendale's, ah had to set a lot of that aside. Not all of it, mind you—ah earn my livin' from my charm. You know, Hillendale's pays well enough, I guess, but the folks there ain't a whole lot of fun. The executives there wash their hands after they drain their lizards. Now that don't make a whole lot of sense, does it?"

I looked at Poorman and blinked.

He grinned. "Down in Texas daddies teach their kids not to go pee-pee on their fingers."

August Poorman believed in doing an honest day's work for an honest day's pay. The Hillendale's people wanted charm, they got charm. I followed the directions on my map and soon we saw the smokehouse—a low, modern-looking building a couple of hundred yards up from the Pacific Ocean.

Poorman smiled. "Y'all suppose they always had smokehouses like this, Mr. Denson? I mean when Captain Grey sailed up the Columbia and all."

The SalPacInc smokehouse and cannery was a building of uninspired, cheapskate modern—it could have been a motel, a minimum-security prison, or a schoolhouse, depending on your imagination. "Times change," I said.

"As long as the salmon is what they say it is, that's all I care, Mr. Denson. I don't care for fish stories, if you know what I mean."

Jim Davis, the man in charge of the reservation smokehouse, had been warned that the man from Hillendale's was on his way. He was at the front door to meet us, clipboard in hand. He wore blue jeans, a brown tweed jacket, and a western string tie. He had a long black pigtail running down the back of his jacket. He was not a full-blooded Indian. His eyes were a disconcerting green.

"Mr. Denson. Mr. Poorman." Davis shook our hands solemnly. If the SalPacInc smokehouse sold to Hillendale's, its owners had a ready-made endorsement for their advertising. "If you gentlemen will wait here a moment I'll tell the people out back that you're here. We ordinarily don't have visitors. We've got too much work to do. We've had a few mechanical problems lately, but we've got that squared away."

Davis walked quickly down a hall, opened a door, and said something to whoever was inside.

Poorman said to me, "It may be true that he doesn't look like he stepped off a nickel, Mr. Denson, but remember, the salmon's the thing." When Davis returned, Poorman said, "Could you tell us your marinade formula, Mr. Davis? I've been told the secret of good smoked fish is the marinade."

"And the wood you use," Davis said. "I'm sorry, I won't be able to give you the recipe for the marinade. In this case it's a tribal secret; it's why our fish is better than the next guy's. You wouldn't want us to give away something like that, would you?"

Poorman looked thoughtful and adjusted his Stetson. White folks paid top dollar for mystique. "I see," he said.

"I can take you to the smoking hodge," Davis said. He gave Poorman his clipboard. "As you can see, these fish are all caught by Indians. We log in the fisherman's name and the time and place the fish was caught." Davis waited while Poorman examined the chart. "We feed all this information into a computer and it helps us increase the catch from year to year."

I said, "You wouldn't happen to buy fish from the Prettybird brothers, would you? Willie's a dart-throwing friend of mine."

Davis cleared his throat. "Why, yes, I've bought fish from Willie and Rodney."

Poorman gave the clipboard back to his host. "I take it I can buy a few fish to sample before I place a larger order for my clients."

"Certainly," Davis said. "We ordinarily don't like people going in and out of the smokehouse because it changes the humidity. We do our best to re-create the interior of a traditional smoking hodge, Mr. Poorman, but we do have state and federal sanitary regulations to follow. I'm sure you understand."

"Damn government's everywhere, that's a fact," Poorman said.

"We use only hardwoods indigenous to the Pacific Northwest," Davis said. "That's guaranteed, as is the authenticity of our marinade." He was calm in the presence of a Hillendale's buyer, I granted him that. We followed him down the hall to the door opposite the one he had opened earlier. Inside the smoking hodge, a conveyor belt of heavy-gauge wire screen emerged from the smoking chamber.

"We move our salmon in and out of our smoke hodge on this conveyor belt so as to reduce handling by human hands. When one of our customers orders a whole smoked salmon, he wants it to look like a salmon. Cooked fish doesn't hold up under a lot of handling."

"We don't sell food that don't look handsome," Poorman said.

Davis looked solemnly at his clipboard. "Now, then, Mr. Poorman, as you will see, each one of these fish is identified by a large numbered tag. I'll start the conveyor belt, and as the salmon come out of the smoke and pass by us, I'll give you the identifying data of each fish and you can select or reject them as you please. The choice is up to you. The fish I'm showing here are our best; they're line-caught, by the way." Davis, too, had read the blurb in the Hillendale's catalog. All three of us knew the line-caught business was nonsense.

"We want the best," Poorman said. "Y'all've got quite a setup here."

Davis pushed a small red button and the wire belt started moving. We watched the first salmon emerge from the smokehouse.

"Okay, now this first fish—fish number one—is an eighteen-pound Chinook caught by James Whitewater just off Moclips yesterday afternoon. James is a Quinault. Do you want the time on that?"

"You can skip the times. Good-looking fish. I'll take it," Poorman said.

Davis apparently needed reading glasses, because he held the clipboard in front of him at nearly arm's length and squinted. "Fish number two was also caught off the mouth of the Columbia by Rodney Prettybird, a Cowlitz." Davis glanced at me. "This is a coho, or what we call a silver here in the Northwest. This one's eight pounds. These smaller fish can sometimes be the best. Hillendale's would be getting chinook only, however—no silvers."

"I'll take that one, too," Poorman said.

So it went, all the identifying data as the fish passed by on the belt. Augustus Poorman bought four fish. Then, he said, "If we could also see the canning facilities."

"Certainly," Davis said. He led us to the far end of the building, into a large, steamy room, with shiny cans moving herky-jerky along a cable that had supports on either side to keep the cans upright. "Here's our canning room. We have the latest, most up-to-date canning equipment—imported from Sweden. Everything exceeds federal safety standards."

"You have to be careful when you're talking canned fish," Poorman said. He didn't need to mention the Alaskan botulism that had financially destroyed a cannery.

"Believe me, we're careful," Davis said. "We've got our reputation."

"Mr. Denson here is gonna have to give a report to our insurers—do you suppose you could take us right up to the line there? Let us take a look."

Davis nodded and led the way to cans of smoked canned salmon as they inched their way to the sealer machine that slapped a lid on then made a little *whump-huff* sound. It went *whump-huff, whump-huff, whump-huff,* as the cans went through one, two, three.

Poorman said, "You might want to examine a few cans at random, Mr. Denson; you want to be able to include that in your report. Looks impressive there."

"Help yourself," Davis said. "As you can see, we're generous with the fish. We're not selling cans of water. We let other people do that."

"How long before this gets on the market?" Poorman asked.

"Once these cans go through the labeler there, we box them and put them on the truck. We deal in quality fish. We don't let it back up and stand around. You'll be able to buy these cans tomorrow afternoon at the Pike Place Market or in your better shops."

I noticed he said shops, not markets. You had to have a few bucks to spring for this fish. I picked up a can and examined the contents, although I didn't have any idea what I was supposed to be looking for. I tried not to breathe or shed dandruff or something. It looked like good salmon to me. It certainly smelled good. I handed it to Augustus Poorman and he looked at it also. He insisted on being dramatic with each can, lingered over it, peering at each close up, like he really knew his stuff. We went through this boring charade for ten or twelve cans before I'd had enough.

The whole thing was so dumb. I should have known something was wrong. What kind of Texan is it who takes five minutes to examine a can of fish? For that matter, what kind of Texan is it who wears gloves all the time? Texans want to show off the domestic crude under their nails. A man from Hillendale's wearing a white Stetson? That was just a bit much, if I'd really thought about it.

15 FOXX JENSEN

I drove Augustus Poorman to Olympia, where he could make airline connections to New York, and turned south on I-5, listening to reports of a frozen foot being found in the Pioneer Place. Thanks to the Hillendale's assignment, I was already sixty miles south of Seattle, and there was no reason I could see not to take advantage of a head start. I drove to Ilwaco at the mouth of the Columbia River, a rainy three-hour grind; I wanted to talk to William "Foxx" Jensen, champion of the sport fisherman.

It was easy to find Jensen's motel; Foxx Jensen's Chinook Inn was the largest and newest in Ilwaco and had a fine view of the fishing harbor. The windows of the Inn's restaurant were steamed from the warmth inside; it looked charming, welcoming, a cozy refuge from the cold mist. I shook the rain off my Irish walking hat and opened the door to the smell of frying Walla Walla sweets and the muted *clunk clunk* of dishes in the kitchen. The tables and chairs were made of varnished knotty pine; there were elks' antlers on the walls, stuffed pheasants, stuffed mallards and chukkers, mounted chinooks and silvers. Some of the fried onions were crammed inside cheeseburgers on the tray of a waitress on her way to a table of fishermen.

"Those onions smell good," I said. "I'm looking for a man named William Jensen."

The waitress smiled. "The onions on that grill sell a lot of cheeseburgers. Everybody calls him Foxx. He and George just got in from Seattle." The waitress motioned to an enormous fireplace in the main dining room. The fireplace was made of Oregon rainbow, a rose-colored stone streaked with lavenders, yellows, and greens.

The redoubtable Foxx Jensen himself, gentleman and sportsman, sat in a rocking chair drinking a cup of coffee and stroking the belly of his affectionate dog. It was the same dog who had been at his side when I saw him on television. The grateful dog turned on his back. He smiled a dog's smile; his brown eyes turned to look at me, but his head never moved.

Jensen was in his late forties. His neck rose from his shoulders like one of Mike Stark's Chanterelle mushrooms. His face, colored by wind, sun, and bourbon whiskey, looked like a freshly scrubbed red potato. He wore a wool shirt with large red-and-black checks, like sportsmen wear in *Field & Stream* magazine. I gave him my line about representing a life-insurance company. He rolled his eyes and grinned a lopsided sardonic grin.

Jensen waved at his waitress. "Another cup for me and one for my friend here. Sure, Mr. Denson, I'll tell you what you want to know. We don't have anything to fear from the truth. The truth never hurt anybody. Ain't that right, George?" He gave the dog a pat. "Little more truth and we'd all be better off."

"The truth is all I'm interested in."

Jensen shook his Chanterelle neck vigorously, with much sincerity. "Glad you came down, Mr. Denson, I mean that. There's so much bullshit about this so-called 'Indian rights' business that you just wouldn't believe it. Oh, George, George." He rubbed the dog's belly.

I sat down and accepted the coffee.

"George's a hunter. He points. He retrieves. He does everything. He's a German shorthair. There's no reason to feed a big lummox of a dog. The breeders got smart, started moving toward smaller dogs. You just love the water, don't you, George?" Jensen stroked George's upturned belly. "I've been up in Seattle talking to reporters and the television people. I want to tell you something about this fishing hoorah that's a fact, Mr. Denson. If you take into account what people spend in motels and restaurants, sportsmen spend about thirty bucks for every fish they take out of the water. Thirty bucks! You can troll a lot of damn lures in the water without destroying the salmon run. If we sportsmen weren't organized, there wouldn't be a damn salmon left in these rivers."

"My client may have to pay Judge Rappaport's wife an interim sum until he returns or we know what happened to him. This is just a routine investigation. The company's officers just want an idea of the possibilities. You know how it is."

"No use forking over a lot of money if you don't have to, eh?" Jensen said. "Say, how would you like some apple pie with a big wad of ice cream on top? The sign outside says our pies are homemade, which isn't technically true, but it's close. We make 'em in the kitchen." Jensen closed his eyes and smiled at the thought of Foxx Jensen's homemade pies. "No bakery crap. None of that. A couple of apple pie à la mode!" he called to his waitress. He said to me softly, confidentially, man to man, "I got me a kid back there with greasy hair and pimples, see, damnedest looking specimen you ever seen. But he carries his weight; he's got a way with lard and flour." Jensen glanced proudly in the direction of the kitchen. "We make him wear a hairnet, but I've never met the granny yet who could match his pies."

Having told me about his pies, Foxx Jensen was ready to talk business. He said, "What do you know about Indians, Mr. Denson? Do you know why they bury Nisquallys with their butts up?"

I had to be Jensen's kind of guy if I wanted him to open up. "Beats me," I said.

"Bicycle racks for Puyallups!" Foxx Jensen laughed a deep, rolling laugh. He accepted his apple pie. "Taste them apples. Don't they smell sweet? Smell that cinnamon. 'Course we have to charge a little for slices like this. If we didn't people'd start coming in here with their runny-nosed kids. Say, do you know how to tell if a Cowlitz has been through your backyard?"

"Haven't heard that one," I said. I'd have to remember these for Willie Prettybird.

"Your garbage can's empty and your dog's pregnant." Foxx Jensen laughed. His dog rolled over to better receive the heat of the fire.

"Do you know of any reason why anyone would want to do the Prettybirds harm?" I said.

Jensen wiped a residue of ice cream from the corner of his mouth. "Do them harm? The Prettybirds? I wouldn't mind putting them in the happy hunting ground. What're you think-ing—someone might of kidnaped Rappaport and blamed it on the Cowlitz? Is that it? Why?" Jensen looked at me like I was nuts. "You want to know the truth? The truth is government never signed a treaty with the Cowlitz but the Prettybirds want to pretend it did. All Rodney wants to do is sit on his ass like the Puyallups and bitch about how he and his brother're supposed to have the right to stretch their goddamn nets across the mouth of the Columbia River. Their 'usual and accus-tomed' fishing grounds. Ooohhhh!" Jensen shook his head angrily. "They want half the fish

going to the Cowlitz. Half! Can you imagine
that? Old Rodney can't wait to have a bunch of
boats out there scooping up fish. Well, those so-
called treaties were signed a hundred and
thirty years ago. Times change. Rappaport may
be nuttier than a fruitcake, but he's nobody's
fool."

"I suppose that is a lot of fish," I said.

"A lot of fish? You bet it's a lot of fish! The
Prettybirds've spent thousands of dollars on
this lawsuit. You have to ask yourself why. Old
Willie's a clever son of a bitch, I'll give him
that. Might as well be white for the way he
acts. What he's got in mind, you see, is cornering
the salmon market like some damn Arab sitting on all the oil. Hell, if Rappaport let the
Prettybirds have their way, people in Portland
and up in Seattle'd be paying fifteen bucks a
pound so a bunch of Redskins could drive
Cadillacs and sit around watching TV off'n
satellite disks."

"They apparently do stand to make some
money."

"You know, they scooped fish up in traps
until we made them knock it off in 1934. Did
you know you could catch every salmon entering the Columbia if you use traps? Every
goddamn fish! We stopped that, and now they're
whimpering they're entitled to half the salmon.
I say again, they want half the fish? Half! Do
you have any idea of how many people drive
down here to have a good time with a fishing
rod? Do you? Listen, this country belongs to us

all. The salmon belong to us all. It's a common resource. If you suspect the Prettybirds of being mixed up in this Rappaport thing, I can see why."

"Some threats were made on one of the Prettybirds," I said.

"Old Rodney, I'll bet."

"This was told to me in confidence," I said.

Jensen finished his apple pie and cleaned his lips with his tongue. Jensen grinned. "It was Rodney. Listen, that young buck's got his problems. A man with a temper like that gets himself in trouble sooner or later. People'll only put up with that 'Native American' crap so long. If he keeps it up, it'll come back on him, you mark my word. If you want to talk about the Prettybirds then you ought to be talking to Doug Egan. You want to talk hardcore, talk to Egan."

"He's the commercial fisherman."

"Shit, Doug Egan ain't no damn fisherman. You call that fishing! He's no better than the Prettybirds. Rodney Prettybird at least gets out on the water once in a while. You say you want the truth, Mr. Denson? The truth is, Egan inherited his boats from his father-in-law. He's got this wife with big tits, and he just fawns over her. He's pussy-whipped, is what he is. Doug Egan corks Rodney Prettybird's nets for the sole reason he doesn't like competition. All his pissing and moaning about fishing being his way of life. You'd think he was born in the middle of the Columbia River bar in a squall.

Balls! His old man managed a Fred Meyer's in Portland. He grew up in Lake Oswego." Jensen looked scornful. "It was his wife's family's way of life, maybe, but never his. He doesn't care if the Indians have treaty rights on the Chehalis or the Nisqually or the Skagit or the Nooksack. That's somebody else's problem. Egan just doesn't want 'em down here in the Columbia. He thinks this is his water, brother, and don't let him tell you any differently."

"I probably should talk to Egan."

"If you want the full range of possibilities." Jensen lowered his voice and gave me a conspiratorial wink. "You should drive to Astoria just to take a look at Egan's wife. Man, I bet she throws a wild screw. Beats me how she could marry a guy like that. Look, you want to know the truth about Doug Egan?"

"Well, sure . . ."

"Doug Egan's a lying pussy."

"With a good-looking, rich wife."

"Oh, yes. She's got bucks all right. And what do they spend it on? See if you can talk to him at his home, Denson; you'll see what I mean."

"Good-looking house too, eh?"

"House? No, that's okay, I guess. Bit show-offy. It's the fish I'm talking about. I won't tell you though, you'll have to see them for yourself." Jensen slapped his thigh. George the dog, momentarily sated from the heat, wiggled for more attention from Jensen's hand. "World is full of screwballs, Denson. Ain't that right, George?" Jensen nudged the dog's ear. The dog gave Jensen an adoring look. Jensen said, "Old George's a hunter, ain'tcha, George?" He was proud of his dog. "Yes, he's a smart one, he is." He ruffled his ears for him.

"I don't think I've ever seen a real hunting dog work."

Jensen beamed. "You should see George. He's worked pheasants, chukkars. He once cleared a barbed-wire fence chasing a crippled honker. He'll fetch a pintail from halfway out in the Columbia and not even be breathing hard. He's a natural. Give me a couple hours and I'll train him to fetch a paper, lead a blind man across the street, you name it. He was bred smart."

"I don't think I'd ever have the patience to train a dog," I said.

Jensen said, "No problem with George. None at all. Hell, me and George're inseparable. He goes everywhere with me, just loves the front seat of the pickup. Sits right up there. Ain't that right, George?" Jensen grinned. He stroked George's throat. George closed his huge brown eyes. The fire was warm. Jensen's touch was gentle. George was in ecstasy.

It was a fact that Foxx Jensen was proud of his dog. If he was a liar in other matters, he was a good one; I'll give him that.

Before I left, I phoned Doug Egan's home in Astoria and a deep-voiced man said sure, drive on over. He'd love to talk. He said he wanted me to meet his wife. "I'll show you my fish.

Everybody likes my fish. But you probably know all about them?"

"Your fish?" This must have been what Jensen was talking about.

"Sure! Some people from a Japanese television network came here and took pictures of them."

My stomach growled. I was hungry but I didn't want to eat at Foxx Jensen's. I wanted some privacy where I could think. I looked at my wristwatch. "Would it be okay if I got there, say, about three o'clock," I said. I figured that'd give me enough time for lunch and the drive to Astoria.

Egan said, "Sure, sure, Mr. Denson. Take your time." These fishing folk were warm people.

Two deep-voiced men in one day—first Poorman and now Egan. That was some kind of omen, I was sure of it.

As I was driving out of Ilwaco I saw the other half of the omen get out of a car at a gas station and put on a big white Stetson. The little sport saw me and took his hat off quick as a ferret. What was Augustus Poorman doing in Ilwaco? He didn't work for Hillendale's, that was for certain. I'd been had. Just how, I wasn't sure.

16 MR. AND MRS. EGAN

It was hard to get Augustus Poorman and his white hat off my mind as I drove along the Washington shore of the Columbia River and crossed the bridge to the Oregon side at Astoria. The Lewis and Clark explorers spent a cold and wet winter not far from Astoria. Later, the small harbor just inside the mouth of the Columbia was the site of a trading post run by John Jacob Astor for the Hudson's Bay Trading Company. Finnish and Norwegian immigrants eventually moved in, and Astoria became a fishing town. People fished there or worked in canneries that packed tuna and salmon.

Doug Egan wasn't a Finn or a Norwegian, but he earned at least a few bucks, judging from his restored Victorian house that sat high on a bluff overlooking the town and the river beyond. The house was freshly painted, a handsome thing, immaculately restored. But few houses could compete with Egan's fish. The huge wooden salmon were something else again; I understood the curiosity of the Japanese television people.

The salmon, sculpted by a chainsaw from huge logs of Douglas fir—each one was maybe ten or twelve feet long—were lined up in the center of a long, gently curving sidewalk, a series of terraces, actually, that rose slowly rather than quickly as stairs would. Each huge, twisting fish leaped upward to the next terrace, as though—like a real salmon—it was struggling to reach the fresh waters of its birth.

This was the final act of life's cycle for a salmon, a private moment carved by a chainsaw. But each fish was cold, inert, frozen in time— rather like an ice sculpture of a woman at the moment of orgasm. A visitor walked on one side of the fish going up, on the other side coming down. There were twenty of them.

There were well-tended gardens of bonsai evergreens on both sides of the sidewalk or rapids or whatever it was supposed to be. I adjusted my Irish walking hat, turned my back on the rain that drifted in with the wind, and rang the doorbell.

Doug Egan answered, a man with a powerful voice, heavy eyebrows, and a jaw that probably never looked cleanly shaved. "Won't you come in, Mr. Denson? Get out of that rain. Brrrr! Here, let me take your coat. Annaliese! I want you to meet my wife, she's wonderful." I'd never seen, outside of television ads, a man as cheerfully domestic.

Annaliese Egan, a tall blond woman with breasts like Cadillac bumpers, said hello, pleased to meet you, and took my coat and hat. It was hard not to stare. Nothing imagined by Vargas could compete with Mrs. Egan's mammaries. They belonged in a museum. Up close and devoid of a tan, they must have looked like ski slopes.

When Egan's wife had disappeared, he said, "Finnish tits! Aren't they something? She could float on her back in a typhoon."

I didn't think I'd stared. I'd tried not to. I'd done my best.

Egan laughed. "You were very cool, I have to hand it to you. But everybody wonders. You can't blame them. I know I would. Before we go into my study, let me tell you about my fish." We stood before the large picture window that overlooked the bluff with the fish and the river below. "Those are chainsaw sculptures, you might have heard of them. A lumberjack in Clatskanie did these. He cut the trees, hauled in the logs, and buzzed 'em into fish. The damnedest thing you ever saw."

"They're beautiful," I said, and meant it. They were beautiful in the way my stuffed-bulldog doorbell was beautiful, but I don't think Doug Egan looked at it that way.

"You know, the art instructor over at the community college said these were indig— indig—what the hell is that word?—kind of art."

"Indigenous," I said.

"That's the word, in-dig-en-ous." Egan pronounced it slowly. "The art instructor said baseball started at Cooperstown, jazz started in

New Orleans, and chainsaw sculpting comes from right here in Oregon. This guy in Clatskanie is one of those great big lumberjacks, you know, with corked boots and suspenders. He came out here with a grin on his face and went *bbbzzzttt! bbbzzzttt! bbbzzzttt!* with his chainsaw on those logs—sawdust flying—carving salmon while his little girlfriend looked on, as proud and pleased as she could be. The art instructor said this lumberjack's a chainsaw Rodin." Egan made the chainsaw sound by buzzing his lips. He obviously took pride in his imitation. He pronounced Rodin Ro-din, as in no sin.

"Well, sure."

"You know, after he was finished with the fish, I had to have a chainsaw, too. Went out and bought me one. Cutting a fir tree's like going through butter." Egan liked to make chainsaw noises. He went, *"Bbbzzzttt! Bbbzzzttt! Bbbzzzttt!* You got yourself three slices of wood. Damndest things." He led me into his study, which was decorated with photographs of weathered fishermen on their boats and repairing their nets. We could see Egan's famous fish leaping their way up the hill to our left. Annaliese brought us coffee. Any more coffee and I was going to get the jitters. I was determined not to so much as glance at Mrs. Egan's deservedly renowned chest.

"The damn things cause her back problems," Egan said, when she was gone. "Boy, I miss her, you know. I've been spending most of my time in Seattle lately, on this Cowlitz suit.

We've filed a brief as friends of the court."

"We?"

"The commercial fishermen's association. Somebody's got to protect the public interest."

"Judge Rappaport had a life insurance policy payable to his wife," I said. I let Egan finish the sentence.

"And you're with the insurance company." Egan's deep voice was remarkable.

"Yes, I am. You should be on the radio with a voice like that."

Egan laughed and smoothed back his eyebrows with the tips of his fingers. "That's what they say. Listen, Mr. Denson, if you people suspect foul play, I'd take a long, hard look at Willie and Rodney Prettybird. That's if I were you. Yes, sir."

"I want to talk to everybody involved, Mr. Egan."

"You know if the Prettybirds get treaty rights down here, they're going to start putting people out of business. That's what happened on the rivers on the Washington coast. In 1974 George Boldt gave the Indians half the fish in their 'usual and accustomed' fishing grounds. The do-gooders just love to throw around that 'usual and accustomed' crap." Egan exhaled between puffed cheeks. "Usual and accustomed! You want to talk about usual and accustomed? My wife in there, Annaliese, well, let me tell you her family's been fishing in Astoria for a hundred years. The courts all of a sudden handed the fish over to the Indians. Do you

know what Boldt did? Do you?" Egan leaned
toward me, his voice getting deeper, gruffer.

"I'm not sure," I said.

"He damned near killed the fishing industry
in the state of Washington, that's what he did.
Before you know it, we'll all be starving to
death on bottom fish. The poor bastards in
Washington had to go to Alaska. It just goddamned near killed off a way of life." Egan
looked at my coffee cup, which was half empty.
"Say, what do you say we fix these up?" He slid
open the door of a teak liquor cabinet and spiked
our coffee with some Wild Turkey whiskey.

I couldn't believe he'd used Wild Turkey in
coffee. "What happened in Alaska?"

"The Alaskan government put a stop to it.
You had to buy a licensed boat to fish in
Alaskan waters. Jimmy Carter's people bud-
geted some money to buy the equipment of
people who were put out of business, but that
ended with Ronald Reagan. The noble Native
American! Bullshit!" Egan looked out of the
window at the rain and clouds that moved up
river from the mouth of the Columbia. Egan
said, "You talked to that old liar Foxx Jensen, I
take it."

"Just this morning."

"He take you out on one of his boats?"

"He has boats?"

Egan stood and called in the direction of the
kitchen. "Annaliese, honey, could we have some
coffee in here." Egan turned to me and lowered
his voice. "Cheap cocksucker! He could have at

least offered to take you out on the water.
William 'Foxx' Jensen as he calls himself—with
two phony X's—has ten, count 'em, ten boats
out there dragging lures around for sportsmen."

"Well!" Curious that Jensen hadn't told me.

"He tell you about his little move to grab
that cannery up there on the coast?"

"That would be?"

"SalPacInc, on the Quinault Reservation. Nobody knows how to kiss-ass better than William Jensen. Why do you suppose they call him
Foxx? For years, he's been giving discounts to
bankers who want to try their luck with the
chinook. The old Foxx loves his bucks, loves 'em.
He sits there in his restaurant scratching his
goddamned dog—probably sleeps with the
damned thing. He got some of those money
boys to go in with him to buy out SalPacInc."

Which no doubt accounted for Augustus
Poorman's appearance in Ilwaco. The old Foxx!
"What happened?" I asked.

Egan watched while his wife poured us more
coffee. "Isn't she wonderful?" he said, as she
handed me my cup. What could I say? Egan
said, "What happened was that Willie and
Rodney Prettybird got a loan from the Small
Business Administration—minorities and all that
crap—and made a bid for the cannery. Why do
you think they want treaty rights for the
Columbia? They could either move the cannery
down here or truck the fish up there; no big
deal either way. Can't start a cannery from
scratch, though—too much money these days."

Willie and Rodney wanted to buy SalPacInc? Why hadn't Willie told me? "Who owns SalPacInc?"

"It's mostly owned by a halfbreed named Davis. He'd probably have sold out to Jensen if the Prettybirds hadn't made an offer. Now he's just sitting back and taking it easy."

"Just watching the price go up."

"That's about it. I don't think the Prettybirds can keep up, though." Egan looked amused. "Maybe the fuckers'll go bankrupt." He could hear his wife talking on the telephone in the kitchen. "Isn't she just fabulous?" he said, in his deep radio announcer's voice. Doug Egan had a wife with a famous front and the money to stake him to a fishing business. He was so secure that he seemed not to be showing off when he wasted Wild Turkey bourbon by pouring it into coffee. He had world-famous Douglas fir salmon leaping up the sidewalk to his handsome home. But he wasn't satisfied; he wanted more. He lowered his voice to a whisper. "Just between you and me, Mr. Denson, I'm not the kind of guy to get fucked over by a young buck like Rodney Prettybird without fucking back. You understand what I mean?"

Doug Egan's hormones prevented him from keeping his intentions to himself, which would have been the smart thing to do. He just had to tell me what was on his mind. Had to.

17 DOWN AT THE STATION

I knew who they were when I saw them coming up the sidewalk. They had that look about them. Something about their walk. Casual. In charge. They wore raincoats and their shoes were polished. Cops. One was tall and dark-haired, the other broad and blond. They looked about them as they walked, appraising the condominium building. They were thinking: this guy Denson's a private, true, but he has a roof over his head. At one time or another each one of them had probably wondered if he shouldn't try it—go private, starve on freedom.

I suspected I was going to learn the truth about Augustus Poorman. Poorman either worked for Foxx Jensen or Willie Prettybird. These gentlemen, I knew, were my payment for not being careful.

I poured myself another cup of coffee, picturing their progress in my mind's eye. They would open the glass door in front, would turn left in the foyer, would smile to themselves as they looked down the hall and saw Winston waiting for them. They would have been talking about Winston on the way over, because he was known by most detectives in the department.

For their entertainment, I selected a bark that sounded like an effeminate Chihuahua—a languid, lisping little bark—a response that hardly fit the terrible Winston. Both cops were laughing when I opened the door with my little punch-button selector in hand.

"You think that one's good, try this," I said. I punched up the blood-curdler with which Winston had greeted Janine Hallen. "He's got five different barks."

The tall one dug his boxtops out of the inside of his jacket pocket and showed them to me, still grinning and staring at Winston in disbelief. The I.D. said he was a Seattle police detective.

He said, "We got a guy at the station who wants to talk to you, and ordinarily he would have come out himself but he broke his foot trying to roller-skate with his kid."

The broad one said, "So he wants to know if you won't let us take you in for a few questions."

"About what?"

"This and that," the tall one said.

I hadn't done anything illegal. "Do I bring my toothbrush?"

The tall one laughed. "No, no. Nothing like that. Just questions, is all. Like I say, he would have come out himself but couldn't on account of his foot. You're not gonna have to have a lawyer with a writ or anything like that."

"Sure, if you bring me back," I said. I got my hat and coat.

We talked about the Sonics' streak on the way down to the police station. The cops were cordial but didn't want to talk about whatever it was I was about to be questioned for. I was taken to the office of Lieutenant Daniel Harner, a freckle-faced man with red hair and his foot in a cast. Harner was middle-aged and paunchy, friendly as an old pair of jeans. He reminded me of Gutley, a shaggy old Chesapeake Bay retriever I'd owned as a kid. Harner looked up from an elaborate model of an old farm that he was building on a table. Everything that was on it was an impeccable miniature.

Harner shook my hand warmly. "Thank you for agreeing to come down, Mr. Denson. I would have driven out myself but I banged my foot up a little. My wife was nagging me about doing more with my kid, so I bought these roller skates for sidewalks at a garage sale—you know those deals with polyurethane wheels and all. I used to skate when I was young, but all I managed to do was break my ankle ten minutes out."

"Ouch!" I said. "I never learned to skate because I grew up in desert country. No sidewalks on a farm."

"My kid felt bad, you know, and my wife felt she was to blame because she'd been nagging me. I was embarrassed, big-deal father and police detective falls down and breaks his ankle. Then the doctor, he says if I want my ankle to be the way it was I gotta keep my weight off it for six weeks."

"The two detectives said you want to talk to me."

"Listen, there's a Thermos of coffee in that cabinet over there and some cups. Why don't you pour us some?" Harner kept talking while I went for the coffee.

"To be honest with you, Mr. Denson, this ain't the way these kind of interrogations are normally conducted. I've got a partner named Willis who really knows how to behave like an asshole. He's got an expressive face, actually. He can come off any way he wants. What we do is take somebody like you to see Willis and Willis makes a lot of threats and scowls a lot—he's got a hell of a scowl—and in general scares the pee-wadding out of people. We let this go on for a while, then I show up and act all compassionate and sensitive and give the impression I think he's an uncivilized moron. Then I bring the poor guy down here to my office and give him a cup of coffee out of my Thermos. It's a lot more impressive than if the coffee comes out of the department pot down the hall; people are more willing to talk."

"Can you get away with an act like that with women?"

"We used to, years ago. I'd wait until their chins started bouncing before I interrupted— just before they were ready to cry." Harner considered the memory. "It was actually sadistic, I suppose, and we can't get away with it anymore, not with women's lib and all. A female suspect feels safe with a matron sitting there to insure that she's not being pawed or something."

"Probably a good thing in the long run, don't you think?"

"Oh, sure. I never had the heart to work a woman sitting there scared to death with her face all bunched up. So my part of the act involves working on my model here. I'm supposed to find what we want to know—all amiable like. No fuss. Working on the model is the trick, Mr. Denson. People are fascinated by miniature figures. It's like I've got a little world here on my table and they get to watch it grow a little. The deal is, Willis isn't working today and I'm not supposed to be moving around so I'm going to have to start right out with the coffee and the model." Harner leaned over the table and began painting a miniature outhouse with a tiny brush. "When I finish one tableau I auction it off to buy Christmas presents for kids who wouldn't ordinarily get them, and start another. This one's a Colorado ranch of the 1870s. As I understand it, you've already met Willis."

"He was here a few days ago when I brought a listening device in here."

"Willis is a smart cop, but he's pissed off a few people over the years. He's impatient with boneheads."

I was curious about what kind of trouble Willis had gotten himself into. "I understand Lieutenant Willis is in some kind of trouble."

Harner scratched his stomach and looked momentarily tired. "I guess you could say that. He's awaiting a disciplinary hearing. Thanks to the union it's a matter of public record."

"I probably won't go look it up, but I'm curious."

"He's charged with insubordination and disrespect for a superior officer, something like that. What happened was that a captain who plays golf with the chief and who is the godfather of the chief's son screwed up on a common rule of law. The result was that a man we all know raped at least five women is walking the streets free on a legal technicality. Well now, Mr. Denson, we had a detectives' meeting where we were all civilized, peers and all that, and pretended that the captain really hadn't done much wrong, that the judge was an asshole, and so on. You know what I mean. Nobody was going to put his dick on the block . . ." Harner looked chagrined.

"What happened?"

"Willis couldn't take it anymore. With the chief of police standing there being everybody's pal, Richard Willis said the truth was the captain didn't know his ass from a hole in the ground."

"Oh, no!"

"Oh, yes. That was just the phrase he used." Daniel Harner felt truly sorry for Richard

Willis. He'd probably wanted to say the same thing himself.

I changed the subject. "You know, when I was a kid I always wanted a miniature steam engine. I remembered looking in the catalog and wanting one always but they cost too much money."

"That's why I turn my tableau money over to the Christmas fund. How long have you known Willie Prettybird, Mr. Denson?"

"A couple of years. I met him at the Pig's Alley Tavern before it got bought out. We both throw darts."

"And you moved to Juantar's Doie Bar?"

"That's where we go to throw now."

"You're Willie's good friend, then?"

"Sure, you could say that."

Harner squeezed a trace of rust-colored acrylic onto his palette. "Are you working for him now?"

I didn't say anything. "Willie's got unreal nerves come out-dart time."

"How was it exactly that you came to accompany Augustus Poorman to see the SalPacInc cannery? Would you tell me that?"

I told him what happened and my reservations and anxiety about Poorman.

"What's the name of that woman at Hillendale's you talked to?"

"Doris Baldwin." I gave him the number I had called at Hillendale's.

"And now you feel something was wrong?"

"Something. Looking back and all. Little Texan in black gloves. Hillendale's."

Harner leaned close to the table and examined the outhouse carefully. "This is a neat little crapper, isn't it? You've seen outhouses like that, haven't you? Are you a very successful private investigator?"

"I pay the rent, I guess."

He applied another dab of paint, an ochre this time. He looked up at me. "You're a trusting man, Mr. Denson. I suppose in most people that's a fine trait."

"Poorman seemed nutty enough to be true. You know how it is. Am I being suspected of something?"

Harner looked surprised. He turned his attention to the roof of his barn. "Barns like this are too expensive to make anymore, you know. But they're beautiful things. Don't you think so? If a man had a barn like this he had something to be proud of. He could care for his animals and feed his family and have a good enough life. They lifted hay up with this little pulley—it's a lot like the apparatus the Dutch use to get furniture into the upper floors of their houses. No, I don't think you did anything wrong, Mr. Denson, but at first blush it might not seem that way."

"A guy wonders, you know."

"Then you went to talk to Foxx Jensen. Do you know Mr. Jensen well, Mr. Denson?"

"I saw him once on television. This was the first time I'd met him."

"Did you ever correspond with him or talk to

him on the phone? Have any contact with him at all?"

"No."

"What did you talk about down there in Ilwaco?"

"My investigation."

"I see. Have you ever been employed by Foxx Jensen, say, through a third party?"

"No."

"Did you agree to contact him after you left?"

"No again."

Lieutenant Harner began putting his paints away. "Mr. Denson, if I were you I'd be a little more selective in the clients I chose. You should give that some thought."

"Are you talking about Poorman?"

Harner smiled.

"Are we finished?" I asked.

"Oh, I think so, Mr. Denson. I do appreciate your help."

"It was pleasant," I said.

"I really do mean what I said about being careful about your clients, Mr. Denson."

"Do you want to tell me who Augustus Poorman is?"

Harner said, "These acrylics really are wonderful, do you know that? You can thin them out just like watercolor. Water down a red real good, and you can make a model barn look like it's spent forty or fifty summers in the sun."

18 BACK RUB

The tall cop and the broad cop took me home after my session with Daniel Harner. They had gotten tired of talking about the Sonics and got onto the subject of a narc friend of theirs who had gotten shot in the foot on a cocaine bust. The broad cop drove and ignored yellow traffic lights on the way to my place. If the traffic was clear on a red light, he ran it cold.

"I don't like those things, either," I said, as we sailed through the second red. "They just wear out your brakes."

"They get in your way," the broad cop said. "If nobody's coming, what the hell?"

"If you see a man in a necktie casually run a red light it means he's a police detective," I said.

"One of the perks," the tall cop said. "The city doesn't pay us worth a damn. People're all the time saying we're vicious cruds. This is a makeup, Denson. The department says, 'Hey, run all the red lights you want. No sweat!' That keeps us happy and doesn't cost them anything. It's called labor relations. Keeps us from signing up with the Teamsters, which everybody knows is run by the Mafia. Up at the U-Dub they teach courses on that kind of thing."

The broad one slowed for a red light at a crowded intersection. "Would you want the Seattle police department in the clutches of the Teamsters and the Mafia, Denson? Would you? Give us a break."

The tall one said, "I bet you privates have some perks of your own, or else why would you go around wearing blue jeans and corduroy jackets. At least we wear decent shoes."

"Income taxes," the broad one said. "We're salaried employees so the government gets its rip before we get our paychecks. Only Denson here knows for sure how much money he makes in a year."

"That's why I wear jeans and a corduroy jacket," I said.

The tall one said, "Fake 'em out, eh, Denson? All right! That's gotta be it. So what's the deal? You get a job here, a job there. Is that it? Cash is just fine by you. This fiver's for you. That buck's for your Uncle Sam; you put your money in a Swiss bank and wear that getup as a front. Not bad."

"I use a bank in the Cayman Islands. Gives me an excuse to go scuba diving. Look, you guys aren't going to turn me in or anything like that?"

"Hey, it's okay, either one of us'd take that kind of action any day," the broad one said.

Once I got back to my apartment I turned on my radio and tuned into a virtually adless and newsless FM station that played mellow music. The media people were getting all oh-no! and oh-my! over the butcher murder story, which was a bit hypocritical as far as I was concerned. The truth was they loved it. Big-time Pervert! I treated myself to a glass of screw-top red. It was a playful vintage—at least six months old—with an aroma, I thought, that hinted of mildewed vinegar. The first taste of it puckered my mouth and made saliva run in the back of my throat. I got myself some carrot sticks and thought things over. I still didn't know who Augustus Poorman was or how I had been used. Judging from Harner's questions, Augustus Poorman's Ilwaco connection was Willie Prettybird's old nemesis, Foxx Jensen. Apparently I wasn't suspected of any crime, but it was embarrassing to have Daniel Harner think I was dangerously stupid. It was embarrassing and not good for business to have a police detective think that way about me.

What I needed was counsel, I told myself. A friend. Succor. Something like that. I thought of Janine Hallen's intelligence. She was orderly, systematic. Perfect for counsel. There lay warmth and passion beneath Janine's measured exterior, I was sure of it. Perfect for a friend. Grand for succor. Emma at the answering service, who knows me, said I should avoid women like that; I should find a woman who doesn't mind a sink full of dirty dishes. To hell with Emma. I phoned Janine.

"I'm glad you called, Mr. Denson. I was wondering about your adventures. What happened? What did you find out?"

There was hope for succor, I thought, but I had to be careful. "I spent a few hours on the road, Janine. I talked to Mike Stark. I talked to a cop about the bug in Melinda's apartment. I took a salmon buyer from Hillendale's to the coast. I drove down to Ilwaco and talked to Foxx Jensen. I talked to Egan. I was interrogated by the police."

"Interrogated by the police?"

"Just some good old-fashioned sadism. The bastards kept me up half the night, most of it standing with a hot light in my face," I said.

"They what?" She was concerned.

"I'm exhausted. I thought that kind of stuff went out with the movies."

Janine Hallen may have been a lawyer with a Mensa I.Q., but I was convinced that in the heart of most good women there lurks a desire to provide succor to something—a goldfish, a cat, a private detective, maybe. She said, "Is there anything I can do?"

I wanted to say, Was there ever, lady! But I didn't. I said, "Gee, I don't think there's anything you can do. My muscles ache from the standing. Maybe I'll make myself a hot toddy or something. A hot bath might be nice."

"Sue them."

I laughed and thought it sounded genuine

enough. "Oh, that's lawyer talk, Janine. I couldn't do anything like that. I have to deal with these guys in the future. Some times you just have to grit your teeth and take your lumps."

"I think I should go to your place. We should talk this over. I need to know what you found out."

"I don't know if I'm up for a report now. Mostly I need to relax, a back rub or something. Ahh, wouldn't a back rub be nice?" This was a moment of truth; I licked my lips in anticipation.

Janine said, "I do want to talk to you, Mr. Denson."

She hadn't said flat no to the back rub. There was hope. I sighed, a civilized good guy, taking defeat gracefully. "Sure, come on over, Janine. I know you need this information. I'll do my best."

My hormones got me all worked up while I waited for her to arrive. I took a hot shower, going lather, lather, lather with the soap; Janine was so fastidious that I wanted to be as sterile as possible. I doused myself with after-shower lotion—although for my part I like a woman to smell like a woman. My mother had given me the lotion for Christmas five years earlier and I'd never opened it. I thought about shaving again, but then thought better of it. I wanted to look a bit haggard if possible.

Janine Hallen arrived bearing a large bottle of brandy, several small bottles of vitamin pills, and a hot pad. She poured me an enormous slug of brandy and insisted I eat several pills, after which she retired to my easy chair while I stretched out on my couch. "So what were their names?" she asked. "In a case like this you have to know who you're dealing with. The first thing we do is get the details on paper, now, while the whole thing's fresh in your mind."

"Janine, listen. A private investigator really can't go around suing the police. I depend on them too much. Every once in a while I run across some bastard who's envious of my freedom and he takes it out on my hide."

"John, it's your duty to sue. The police shouldn't be allowed to get away with that kind of thing. You owe it to the community, if nothing else. Here, have some more brandy." She got up and brought me the bottle.

I held my glass up weakly. It was good brandy, and I was game for another good slug but didn't want to appear eager. Remain wan, I told myself. Pale and wan, fond lover. I wished I hadn't put on the after-shower lotion. I couldn't stand the smell. I sighed. "It's just a cost of doing business, Janine."

"You look exhausted."

"You would, too, if you had to stand there and answer the same damn questions a couple of hundred times. You have to understand, they're under a lot of pressure from this butcher murder business. God, my back!"

Janine took a small sip of brandy. She looked

determined. Whoa, did she ever have a lovely body! I hoped there would be no stirring of the Biblical loins to give me away.

"There is no excuse for police brutality. None. You know that. I think in a case like this every citizen has a responsibility. You included, John Denson."

"I'll think about it," I said. "Right now all I want to do is get the knots out of my muscles."

Janine looked resigned. "All right, turn over on your stomach. I'll do your shoulders if you tell me what you learned the past couple of days."

I turned over slowly, remembering that I was supposed to be exhausted, and accepted Janine's kneading. It was wonderful. Her thigh was by my hip on the couch; it felt like a warm fire on a winter afternoon.

"You do seem a little stiff," she said.

I spaced out the stories so as to make the massage last longer. I threw in all kinds of details: Willis's bow tie, Augustus Poorman's white hat and black gloves, Jensen's dog, Egan's chainsaw sculptures. How I'd seen Poorman in Ilwaco. Janine stayed with it for twenty minutes. She had surprisingly strong hands. They felt better and better. The presence of her thigh got more and more disconcerting. She smelled marvelous. I went back over my investigation. My mind raced for any tidbit that I might have inadvertently omitted the first time through. I knew I couldn't keep that up all night. I had to take a chance, go for it. "Do you like massages?" I asked.

"I love them."

"I'll give you a short one before you go, how's that? Turnabout's fair trade." I pleaded silently to any gods that might have been listening. Emma doesn't know what she's talking about. Come on, give me a break . . .

Janine hesitated.

I didn't breathe.

"Well, okay. A short one," she said. She looked at me warily and took her place on the couch. I liked her eyes.

I started with the back of her neck and moved onto her shoulders. I made an elaborate effort to seem objective and nonsexual but it wasn't easy. She had sweet, soft down on the back of her neck. I massaged the backs of her arms. Then I started down her back. The heat rose from her body like a sidewalk in August. I suddenly realized, without really thinking about it, that Janine was far less restrained than I had thought. When I slid my hand onto the inside of her thigh, she said, "I thought you said a short massage," and moved her legs to give me more room.

I slid my hand between her legs. The heat was humid, primordial, beckoning. Her odor made me giddy, sent hormones surging. It was hard to breathe. I would have done anything for her. Anything to be inside her.

She moved herself against the back of my hand. "You give good massages," she said.

"Does that feel good?"

"I'll give you a week to take your hand away," she said.

"It might be even better if you took your jeans off."

Janine said, "You think maybe?" She raised her hips and unzipped the front of her trousers.

I slipped her jeans off. She was wearing a pair of see-through red underpants that gave me a tantalizing, hazy, furiously erotic view.

"Like those underpants?" she asked.

"They're great," I said.

She raised her butt, driving me to a frenzy. She had a wonderful body. No man could have desired more. "I thought you'd like them," she said. "The cops didn't mistreat you, did they, John?"

"I talked to a detective named Daniel Harner. Nice guy. Had a broken ankle from skating with his kid. Should I take those things off now? When did you figure that out?"

"Don't be in a hurry there. The minute you said you needed a back rub."

I slipped my hand down onto her place again, marveling at what an extraordinary woman she was—smart, accomplished, yet capable of uninhibited, honest physical play. She turned, suddenly, and began taking off her blouse while I unbuckled my pants.

"I suppose these aren't the largest you've ever seen?" She kissed me softly.

"I like 'em a lot. I like 'em a lot." I wasn't lying. She had fine firm breasts that would look as good in twenty years as they did now. "That business about the cops was just a little fish story," I said. "No harm done, was there?"

"I agree. No harm done. I'm glad you wore your smoking six-shooter shorts."

"Just for you," I said. I slipped them off.

Janine gripped my barrel tightly and grinned mischievously. She could see I was plenty worked up. She ran her other hand under my cylinders and gave them a couple of gentle turns, sending little *click, click* tremors shuttling up and down my spine. "I hope it doesn't go off here in my hand," she said. "Accidents like that are such a waste."

"Oh, it's got a pretty steady trigger. I don't like to waste 'em either," I said. I couldn't help but swallow, doing my best not to discharge by mistake.

"Is it really a six-shooter? That's impressive."

"Well, a one- or two-shooter, usually. Maybe three if the target's right and it gets a chance to cool off between shots."

"Since it's cocked and all, I suppose you want to try it out."

"I was thinking of it mightily," I said.

Janine Hallen settled unself-consciously onto the couch and gave me a wonderful target. She grabbed me by the barrel which had grown to magnum proportions—sort of—and aimed it properly. She was a screamer under fire. As I gunned her down, she arched her spine and moaned most piteously. Then she lay back, exhausted, smiling, game for more. I got three big, booming rounds off that night, blasted her again and again without mercy. It was the first time that had happened in so long I couldn't remember.

The next morning, after the smoke had finally cleared and we were lying back, relaxed, Janine said, "Say, what's the name of that lotion you're wearing, John?"

"Billy Gruff, something like that. Aspen Stud, maybe. They're all the same."

"Do you wear it often?"

"Are you kidding? Wore it for you. Stuff smells like a French whorehouse, whatever that's like."

"Oh, that's good," Janine said. "You might think about staying with your old habits. You probably smell better without that stuff on." She cuddled up a little closer.

19 RENEGADE

According to the radio news, the count was up to two chops, three steaks, a foot, and two slices of buttock. That's a lot of corpse, but if the police had the victim identified they weren't saying who it was. The wire-service reporters were now giving the radio people cute little features on famous butcher murderers. The hall of fame included a Midwesterner named Ed Gein, who was the featured psychopath as I drove over to see the quick-tempered Richard Willis. However, Ed had gone one step beyond Seattle's nut. I remembered jokes about Ed Gein sandwiches when I was a kid.

The folks at the police station were in a serious mood. The public paid cops to keep butcher murderers off the street.

Richard Willis looked trapped and bored in his office. He had been mauling the top of his Styrofoam coffee cup with his thumb. He pursed his mouth in a tight little circle and squeezed so hard his lips turned pale. "Have you been listening to that crap on the radio?" he demanded. "Butcher murderer!" he said scornfully. "Just what we need is for the bastard to think he's some kind of hero."

"You'd think people'd be satisfied with the Sonics' win streak."

Willis scowled. "It sucks."

I shrugged. "I assume you've been watching Pioneer Place Park."

" 'Me'? You mean 'they,' Denson. I don't have anything to do with it. Have they been watching it?" Willis dug his thumbnail into the rim of his cup. "I want to tell you something. They started out with half the goddamn department down there. They've got a couple of so-called Indians on the force, but they look about as much like Indians as Thurgood Marshall looks black. They even brought in a theater professor from the university to put makeup on 'em. They wound up looking like drag queens."

"They should have paid more attention to affirmative action."

"They got a couple of Indian brothers on loan from the force at Sioux Falls. That's South Dakota. They flew 'em in." Willis smirked. "True-blue Redskin cops, fresh off the reservation."

I said, "I get the picture they're on your rear about something."

Willis's face hardened. He looked at me through narrowed eyes. "If I wasn't a good cop these pansies would have had me out of here long ago. They want to drag everybody down to their level of incompetence. The truth is I'm one of the best cops in the department and I'm having to sit this one out."

"Last time I was in here you mentioned something about a departmental hearing." I was curious about Willis's version of his problem.

"They've got some high-blown complaint. The truth is what I'm up for is saying a stupid asshole was a stupid asshole." Willis paused, grinning at a memory. "This is a guy who's the cause of a violent rapist being allowed to walk the streets until he hurts somebody again. Somebody had to say something, for God's sake. The worst thing you can do in a police department, Denson, the very worst, is to be competent. Competence gets everybody agitated. They hop about like starlings crapping on a sidewalk. They crap, heads bobbing, watching one another. When one starling craps, they all crap. When one flies, they all fly. That way everybody's taken care of. When one cop is allowed to be casual in a rape case, well . . ." Willis's voice trailed off. "No damn wonder women are sore at us. You ever watch birds, Denson?"

"I like killdeers and meadowlarks. Solitary birds."

"I know what you mean. The ones who fly in flocks don't like it, though. You have to watch 'em twenty-four hours a day."

"All a male pelican needs is a female pelican. The cops down here aren't all bad. I thought Gilberto was a pretty good cop. I had a decent feeling about Gilberto."

"I agree Gilberto was a solo bird. What

you're really wondering is, what do I have on the line. Let me put it to you this way: as things stand now I'm very apt to be a security guard in a shopping center next month." Willis stopped, as if he'd suddenly gotten an idea. He turned and opened a file drawer and took out what I saw was a printout of the dossier required for my private investigator's license. He read it silently, apparently oblivious to the fact that I was sitting across from him waiting. He looked up at me, down at the file again, then he closed it, grinning. "Why not?" he said. "I'm going to tell you a story, Denson. Break my confidence and I'll figure out some way to have your balls."

I was curious. "I give you my word," I said.

"They sprung for all the Thunderbird these Redskin cops could drink, see. A cop'll drink anything, and them being Indians made it worse. The South Dakotans went down there, got sloshed and listened and watched. Nothing. More and more bullshit in the papers. Every son-of-a-bitching day the media kept hitting the department. We needed help, Denson. Then . . ."

Willis leaned over confidentially. "Some crafty Japs dumped this wonderful machine square in the collective lap of this group of bewildered cops. To them, it was as if the fucking gods had intervened: Toba."

I sat straight up, looked right, looked left. "Toba?"

"A machine. Now they're always hoping

they're gonna find some kind of machine that'll make up for their lack of intelligence and common sense."

"What kind of machine?"

"A Toba, Denson, is a surveillance device made by Toba Manufacturing Ltd. of Kobe. They've been selling them as private security systems for years and now are looking around at the police market. After we got our second chop, or was it a roast of thigh, they called and wanted to know if we wanted to give Toba a try. They'd even send technicians from the Kobe police force, which has had great success with Toba. They'd give us terms, they said. The Grand High Pooh-Bahs said yes."

"The Japanese make wonderful cars," I said.

"What Toba is essentially is a video camera that gives a computer the license numbers of all vehicles entering and emerging from a given street. It works like the scanner in the post office department that reads zip codes. If you cover all streets leading to an inter-section—as is the case with Pioneer Place Park— Toba can tell you what license numbers enter the area, how long they stay, and whether they go left, right, or straight ahead. We can input the names and addresses of all people with vehicles registered in Washington; Olympia has that data on tape. Toba can pull the licenses that are out of the norm of the traffic."

"I suppose Toba gives you the names and addresses of the registered owners."

"From the Olympia tapes. Sure, we get a list

of suspect vehicles, arranged in groups of priority. There's zone red. The best bets. There's a yellow zone. Strong possibilities. And there's a green zone, Denson. Acceptable risk."

"How about blue?"

"We got blue." Willis ran his tongue along the front of his teeth. "The neutral zone. The computer takes into account traffic lights, ball games at the Kingdome, rush-hour traffic— everything. It constantly recalculates how long it takes an average car to pass through the intersection. If there is a sudden surge of usage of an intersection by one particular car, that vehicle may be moved up to a higher risk list. You see what this means, Denson?"

"I sort of get the picture," I said.

"You can buy extras, like maybe you're buying a tape deck for your car or adding a turbo to the engine. For example, you can buy this camera—which we're using—that gives an ear-piercing *whee-woo*, *whee-woo*, *whee-woo* when somebody breaches a designated perimeter—a hallway, say, or a sidewalk. When he leaves, the camera follows him for a block, still going *whee-woo*, *whee-woo*, *whee-woo*. Baby Toba, the captain calls it. Isn't that sweet? The captain's got surveillance teams ready to scramble when Baby Toba squawls the alert and sends the data to the main computer."

"Expensive, I'll bet."

"Oh, yes, it costs. In this case they've set up monitors on five streets leading to the pergola.

If it works, the chief thinks the City Council will spring for the system."

I grinned. "Catch the butcher, get Toba to play with."

"I'll tell you again: if any of this gets in the newspapers, I'll strangle you, Denson. Do you hear me?"

"I hear you. I gave you my word."

"So the word comes down. You know how it goes. The chief leans on the captain; he says produce, Charles. The captain leans on his incompetent lieutenants; he says produce, swine. Use the machine and produce. If the department can make it work to find this killer, the Pooh-Bahs can invite the television people in to tape a Japanese lady technician smiling and with her delicate hand resting on Toba, an expensive but necessary toy to combat crime in Seattle."

"But it hasn't worked."

"Have you heard of anybody being arrested? Four more days and three or four parts have passed and they don't have their man. It was only after we had gotten ourselves into this, Denson, after we'd had the damn thing printing names and addresses in various colored letters, that the Pooh-Bahs realized what would happen if we can't find the guy. If we can't find him and Toba's failure is made public, the computer program might be set back five or ten years."

"All this while you've had to sit here and watch."

"Just one legal phrase short of a full suspension. I'm not supposed to leave the building during duty hours. It's like this is the big game and I'm having to sit it out. God, you wouldn't believe how they're fucking it up. The captain started out okay, what with the Sioux Falls cops. Only once they saw Toba, they wanted a pure Toba victory. The captain said if you have too many cops hanging around the park, you'll spook the nut. That's the beauty of Toba. That's the logic. And he's right, you have to be careful. There's precedent for how to go about it, though. The captain agrees with the chief in these matters because you don't make captain unless you know how to protect your ass and suck some jerk's cock at the same time."

I said, "Maybe you should lie back a little, slide along with the group."

Willis scowled. "That'll be the fucking day. I go to all the briefings, of course. There's nothing in my instructions that says I can't do that. Besides that, it makes them nervous. They know they're stupid bastards. The captain told them the Sioux Falls Indian brothers were in a stupor from drinking all that cheap wine and ordered them pulled."

"I'd think that was part of their cover. You mean to tell me they don't have anybody directly watching the park? Nobody cheating with a pair of binoculars or something?"

"What they've got, Denson, are surveillance teams hidden in the wings, waiting for the Toba to go *whee-woo*, *whee-woo* and tell them they've got a hot one. Let the butcher come to us, the captain says. Each day the stakes increase. . . ."

"That a pun?"

Willis was impatient. He glowered at me. "That's spelled s-t-a-k-e-s, Denson. Instead of cutting his losses and trying a little old-fashioned human intelligence, the chief decides to ride with the gamble. Let Toba do it. The Pooh-Bahs'll catch the guy red-handed one minute and call a press conference the next: here's your butcher murderer. The scuttlebutt around here is that they know the body's Moby Rappaport but are keeping it secret for some reason that probably makes sense only to them. If that's the case, then the killer could very likely have something to do with the salmon industry people."

"It could, I suppose, but this business of freezing a corpse and cutting it up with a saw sounds more psychopathic, I'd think."

"Sure it does. The department shrink ran the facts through a computer and the computer says the M.O. is psychopathic; the killer will keep on delivering body parts to Pioneer Place Park until he runs out of parts or we catch him." Willis put the palms of his hands over both ears and puffed out his cheeks in exasperation. He looked at the ceiling. "My God! Brilliant! Glad you told me that, professor!"

"Toba sounds like a helluva system."

"Denson, there are people in this world who will stand in the pouring rain and not get out their umbrellas unless a machine tells them it's raining. This is perfect for Toba, the chief says, a setup. My aching ass!" Willis slumped in his chair.

"I assume they do have folks working the psycho angle."

"They get the dumbest cops on the force on something like this, because it's the dumb ones who rise in the hierarchy and get the good cases. The thing is . . ." Willis lowered his voice, ". . . I can work the psycho angle myself without leaving this office—all I have to do is check a terminal out and plug it in right there." He pointed at an electrical outlet behind a metal file cabinet. "If I just had one person on the outside to work with, just one decent investigator."

Richard Willis was a desperate cop. I began to see what he was working toward, and my mouth turned cottony.

He said, "One thing I can't do is check out the people involved in the Rappaport salmon case. It would be nice if I could find somebody to work that angle out."

"Me?" I was dumbfounded. I could see how Willis had gotten into trouble.

"I've been a cop for twenty-four years, Denson. A man develops habits after a while; he's changed by his job. I wade in shit, friend, it's my job. That guy out there with the saw and the corpse is throwing it in my face every day—I don't care if I am about to be kicked off the force. I don't like that." Willis was fuming.

"It's their screwup, not yours. Why don't you let them go under?"

Willis ground his teeth together. "The public pays us to use our brains, Denson."

"Your desk's free of listening devices, I take it." Was this the time to bring up the awkward question of the bug I found in Melinda Prettybird's apartment? I decided not.

"It's clear."

"Suppose I agree to help you play John Henry to Toba. What's in it for me?"

I was a little too loose for Willis's taste. "Don't get cute, Denson. I didn't say anything about playing John Henry. If I lay the butcher in their lap, I'll have the simple and sublime pleasure of sticking it up theirs and breaking it off."

"What would that do to your departmental hearing?"

"Hearing?" Willis smirked. "Why they'd have to cancel it, of course."

"And then there's the question of what's in it for me." I was amiable, friendly. All these people and motives were intertwined in some kind of treacherous story. Of course, I wanted to help my friend Willie Prettybird, but even more than that I wanted to know what the story was. We all want to know what the story is—that's why scandal magazines are so popular.

20 PARTNERS

Richard Willis ran his hand slowly across his face and sighed. "I'll tell you what: I can be your friend in the future. Gilberto moved to California; I'm here. For the present, at least, I'm still a detective. I have access to our files. That kind of arrangement has to be a mother lode for an independent like you, out there on your own. I can pull a file just like that." Willis snapped his fingers.

He was right. That kind of friend on the force is worth bucks to a private investigator. "Gilberto and I got on pretty well," I said.

"I got to be a detective lieutenant, Denson, because in the end I'm smart enough not to turn over all my responsibilities to a mother-fucking machine. Some of them, I don't mind, but this is ridiculous."

"I'll have to work with you and for a client at the same time. To my knowledge he's no murderer."

"If your client turns out to be the killer, I expect you to tell me when you find out. I don't know if you P.I.s take any kind of blood oath, but in a case like this I have to have that promise."

I thought briefly of Willie Prettybird. Willie couldn't have had anything to do with it. He couldn't. "I agree," I said.

"Done then," Willis said. "Sometimes I wonder about this city. First they commissioned some fag architect to design that sweetcake pergola like this was Paris or something. Then they stick a totem pole in the ground knowing damn well it was gonna draw Indians like flypaper. What the hell were they thinking of?"

"I don't think this is really the place to discuss something like this, do you?" I gestured to the hallway.

"You're right, and I like that kind of caution." Willis looked at the clock on the wall. He stood and finished the dregs of his coffee. "My shift's officially up—if you call sitting on your butt working a shift. I feel like a little drink. What do you think, Denson? What the hell, it isn't every day a man has an opportunity to snatch his career from the brink of extinction by assholes. I'll buy." He glanced at himself in the mirror on his wall and adjusted his bow tie. "I know a place."

"I don't have a lawn to mow," I said. I followed him down the hall to the police department parking lot outside.

Willis had found a way of fighting back. He had a chance. He was in an expansive, talkative mood. "It's one thing after another, you know that, Denson. I got this purge hanging over my head, and on top of that my wife has a bladder infection. You ever had to put up with a woman with an infected twat, Denson?"

"Well, I don't know," I said.

"My old lady gets these damned infections, see, and starts accusing me of porking Thunder Thighs, that's this old girlfriend of mine. Her doctor says it's from too much humping—like I'm some kind of rutting maniac. What does he want me to do, squeeze my weasel?"

"He probably does, so he figures everybody should."

"So the infection goes from her twat up her urinary tract to her bladder. Her doctor gives her medicine that turns her pee orange. But she complains the infection makes it burn when she takes a leak, so lately she's taken to sitting in a sink full of water. She says soaking herself relieves the burning. It's times like this that makes you wish you had a bathtub." Willis gave me a disgusted look.

"Does the sitting help her out?" I asked.

"If she'd use the kitchen sink, I don't suppose it'd make any difference—that's if you don't mind her peeling potatoes in it later on. The kitchen sink's solid, built right into the cabinet. But no, she's gotta use the one in the john. Yesterday, she managed to rip the pipes from the wall while she was sitting there with her ass in the water, reading Judith Krantz. You're not married, are you, Denson?"

"I'm by myself."

"You single guys have to flog your dog every day; I gotta find time to fix the damned sink. Nobody wins." Willis fell silent. "If she just wouldn't read that awful crap, I don't suppose it'd be as bad."

I listened to the jabber on the police radio as Richard Willis turned into a small bar under the southern end of the Fremont Bridge.

"This place belongs to my brother-in-law," he said, as we stepped into the warmth of the bar. "These guys pour long for me; Denson, you like whiskey?" Without waiting for me to reply, he said, "Two double bourbons on the rocks, Earl."

"I like whiskey," I said.

Willis took a stiff slug when his drink arrived and made a face. "Here's to the spectacle of a good detective having to find a private detective to help him save his job. Isn't this a fine state of affairs? Enough to make a man puke. This stuff tastes miserable, doesn't it? Here's to justice! Here's to a little well-intentioned conniving!" Willis took two more slams of bourbon. "The chief finds it hard to believe somebody managed to slip stuff into that park when it's being guarded by the terrible Toba. It doesn't compute, as they say."

"I don't understand how this thing works at night?"

"Infrared cameras, Denson. The streetlights are all it needs."

"What does Baby Toba watch, exactly?"

"The sidewalks on all three sides of the park

have been programmed as a perimeter. If somebody steps on the sidewalk Toba starts making
its racket. A sudden shadow is all it takes.
Anything. Of course, as I pointed out to the
damned fools at one of their briefings, all the
murderer has to do is give a chop a sling out of
his car window, and there you have it."

"How does Toba get around that?"

"It doesn't, not really. But the Baby Toba
cameras that monitor the sidewalks show the
street as well, so the captain has cops watching
the screens. If they see a suspicious motion
from a passing car they hit a button."

"I see. I suppose Toba then flashes the
licensed owners of all cars in its vision at that
time."

"That's exactly it. All that and they can't get
the butcher. He has to know they're watching
the pergola, but he can't know about Toba.
How in the hell is he beating that camera?
That's the question."

"Easy," I said. "He uses the underground."

"For what? The underground doesn't go under the park. The killer'd still have to surface,
cross a street, and step over the little fence
around the park there."

"Maybe he's got his freezer down there."

Willis shook his head. "They thought of that,
believe it or not. They checked the underground
and all the buildings inside Toba's traffic monitors to make sure there aren't any freezers or
lockers where someone could stash a corpse. I
can't guarantee how good a job they did. They

exalt the mediocre." Willis rubbed his chin. He reached inside his jacket and gave me a sheet of paper. "Here's a checklist I Xeroxed. Look at it now. I can't risk letting you walk around with it. We can't risk walking around with paper."

I looked at the checklist of rooms and businesses searched. I looked for appliance stores. There were none.

Willis said, "The Prettybirds are right up there on the department's list, Denson; I guess you figured that."

"So what about the bug in Melinda Prettybird's apartment?"

"I told you most of mine. You want more, it's your turn," he said.

That was fair. I wanted to know the truth, too. I unloaded. I told Richard Willis everything—my conversations with Willie, with his sister, with Mike Stark, with Foxx Jensen and Doug Egan. I included every detail I could remember in my Augustus Poorman story.

"Do you know a cop named Harner?" I asked. "When I got back he pulled me in for a few questions about my trip to SalPacInc with Poorman."

"Harner did?"

"Oh, yes. Played with a model farm on a table."

Willis smiled. "Harner and I do a Mutt-and-Jeff act. I'm the hard guy. He plays with his model. He's not a bad guy, actually. A bit careful."

"A company man."

"It's the rare one that isn't."

"Judging from his questions, I'd say he's working on a link between Poorman and Foxx Jensen."

Willis was irked. "They never tell me anything around here now. I'm a regular damned pariah. I knew Harner was working on something related to this business. I wasn't sure what."

"Now you know."

"He doesn't suspect you of anything, does he?"

"He said not. He thought I was pretty dumb though."

Willis said, "It sounds like you might have been. I'll talk to Dan and see what it's all about." Willis killed his whiskey double in one chilling pull and waved for two more. "Replace 'em when they're dead," he said to the bartender. "This business gets curiouser and curiouser."

"A real fish story," I said.

"For your own good, don't believe anybody. I mean anybody."

"You say they searched the underground? I still think that has to be the answer. The butcher's got his goodies stored down there."

"I told you already. They took a good hard look at the underground, every sidewalk, every room, every vault. They found nothing. The captain says if cops keep poking their noses around, they're gonna queer it for Toba."

"So they don't have anything."

"*Nada. Nada. Nada.*" Willis's voice rose. He waved his hand angrily. "They've got diddly squat! Half of them don't know their dicks from a gearshift." Willis was sloshed.

"I can't believe they didn't spot one single suspicious person."

"All right, what do you want me to say? Toba put them onto one guy, driving an old car. Thought maybe he threw something out of the window. They lost him in the rain."

"What kind of an old car?"

"Shit, who knows? An old coupe. One of those late thirties numbers."

"A Ford, maybe? Find out for me." I hadn't told him about Stark's car. I didn't remember it until now.

Willis pursed his lips. "I'll find out. But for God's sake call me if you find anything. I'm having to take Gilberto's word on you."

"I might have to bend a few rules."

Willis said, "Listen, man, my cock's two inches from the paring knife. You don't know how many regulations I've twisted in the last hour." He was intense, passionate.

"I can guess."

"Bend whatever you goddamn have to. Laws, elbows, I don't care."

I did, but I didn't say anything. "And if I think Willie Prettybird is behind all this?"

"I can't see how he isn't."

"I think Willie's okay. We were talking about the bug, remember?"

"We were talking about the bug. One second you're going on about how great a guy Willie Prettybird is, and the next you want to know about the bug. The bug was where it was supposed to be, Denson. Some Seattle cops put it there by authority of a court order."

"What?"

"Oh, yes."

"Why?"

"I don't know for sure, but I've got a few ideas. After you were in my office the other day, I looked up the file on Melinda Prettybird's complaints. Did Willie or Melinda tell you who those guys were who got beaten up while they were bedded down with her?"

"I don't think they mentioned the first two. They said the third guy ran a taco place in Tacoma."

"The first one, sleuth, was a kid named Kim Hartwig."

"The missing law clerk?"

"When Melinda Prettybird awarded him the succor of her bed and breast, he was just starting work on an opinion for Rappaport in the case of Cowlitz vs. the United States."

"Oh, shit."

"That's what I'd say if I were you. There's more."

"Lay it on me."

"Hartwig, Denson, is a suspect party in a judicial tampering case."

I said, "And the other party?"

"The guy you talked to in Astoria. The fisherman Doug Egan. I found that much out."

"Whoa! Good old Doug!" I told Willis about Mike Stark's having seen Egan and Hartwig in Ivar's.

"What we're looking at is a giant tub of crabs. Melinda Prettybird may have been doing a little tampering herself. I'm betting that's the reason for the bug in her apartment. All that little squaw has to do is wiggle it a couple of times and blink those big brown eyes. The sound of her zipper'd take Hartwig to his knees. He'd do anything."

"Oh, boy!" I said. What Willis said was true. I wasn't any different from Hartwig. Melinda had blinked those browns at me, all innocence, and I'd believed her every word. Almost.

Richard Willis drove me back to my car, running two red lights on the way. Lucky he was a cop. He'd never have passed a breathalyzer test.

21 OMISSION

The angry cop, Richard Willis, had really laid it on me, no doubt about that. Doug Egan, concerned that the Cowlitz Indians might get treaty rights to salmon entering the Columbia River, befriends a clerk who is drafting an opinion for District Judge Moby Rappaport in the matter of Cowlitz vs. The State of Washington. Egan is suspected of judicial tampering. The clerk, apparently courted by Melinda Prettybird, goes to bed with her and is beaten up for his troubles. The court sees sufficient reason for the police to place a listening device in Melinda's apartment. Conclusion:

Melinda Prettybird was no doubt herself under investigation for judicial tampering.

Neither Willie Prettybird nor his sister Melinda told me that one of the men who had been beaten up was Rappaport's clerk. He was not the second or third man beaten up; he was the first. Were two men, captives of their hormones and Melinda Prettybird's brown eyes, casually thumped on to provide a cover for the first beating?

Who beat up on the men? Rodney Prettybird? Willie? Had my darts partner looked me square in the face and lied to me? Was Willie trying to set himself up with some kind of alibi or cover by asking me to investigate his sister's problems?

Rappaport was missing, presumed by the police to be the butchered, frozen corpse being rationed out in Pioneer Place for the agitation of the city.

Both the Prettybirds and Foxx Jensen had been trying to buy Jim Davis's SalPacInc fish cannery.

Was my trip to SalPacInc with Augustus Poorman some kind of nutty coincidence? I didn't think so. Why me? Why hadn't Willie said anything about the SalPacInc bid? Something was going to happen as a result of my trip to the coast.

I wondered if I'd wind up losing my taste for salmon. Just what the hell was going to happen to me next?

It was time to confer with Janine Hallen again. Before anything else, I had to talk to her.

I met Janine in Callahan's, a loud, noisy bar and restaurant just north of the Kingdome, where you can have a conversation without pretending you're in a library or an Englishman's club.

Janine chucked her first drink down faster than Richard Willis, which belied her shy appearance. "You want to tell me what you found, Mr. Denson?"

I looked at her over the edge of my gin and sucked the juice out of the pickled cocktail onion. "I'll tell you some of what I found. Maybe everything. It depends."

"On what?"

"You lawyers can go into court and defend a woman you know to be a murderer or a man you know to be a rapist, and you justify it on the grounds that everybody needs a good defense. I don't operate that way. I don't work for people I know are crooks. There are investigators who will do that. I won't. That includes the Prettybirds."

"I'm paid to win in court."

"Willie and Melinda Prettybird may not have flat-out lied to me, but if I'm to believe what everybody has told me, they sure as hell didn't tell me everything they should have."

"Will you do yourself and Willie a favor by finding out the truth before you quit? You owe him that much, don't you? He is your friend."

"If I find out he's a liar or a felon, I quit."

"That's all I ask," she said. "Shall we order something to eat? I feel like something to eat—some scallops, maybe, or prime ribs. I'll buy."

"I try not to be sexist when the lady's paying," I said.

Janine grinned. She motioned for the waiter and told him we'd like a table for two.

"That'll be about a fifteen-minute wait," the waiter said.

"No rush," she said. "Name's Hallen."

While we drank another round and waited for our table, I told Janine Hallen what I had learned, including the inexplicable failure of Toba. She was quick. I'm not proud. I take help wherever I can get it. "So what do you think?" I asked.

"I'm representing the Prettybirds' Cowlitz fishing-rights lawsuit. If Willie and Melinda are involved in some kind of felony, that's something entirely different. I'm like you; I don't like clients lying to me or holding out on me."

"You're curious about how all this fits, then?"

"Sure. Only I don't think that body has anything to do with the Prettybirds, even if it is Moby Rappaport. But if you want me to help you figure it out, I'm game."

I gave her my self-deprecating John Denson smile. "Ms. Hallen, I need all the help I can get. A free dinner. The use of your intelligence. I'll take whatever I can get."

A woman on an intercom said, "Hallen, table for two." I followed Janine Hallen into the dining room.

She glanced at the menu, apparently made up her mind, and said, "The police have checked the underground, I take it."

"The entire labyrinth, all of it. Clear."

"And above ground?"

"On both sides of all three intersecting streets. They found nothing. All the cops know is that the parts are frozen solid. The killer either has to have the body frozen right across the street from the park or he's smuggling the parts in."

Janine Hallen ordered herself some salmon. I went for a large prime rib. "You knew I'd want to help, didn't you?" she said.

"Had an idea you would."

"So you drew a map of the area and named the streets."

"How'd you guess?" I spread a primitive map I'd drawn out on the table while Janine waved for more bread.

"I don't see any appliance stores," she said.

"There aren't any. No freezers, if that's what you're thinking."

"What's this?" She pointed to a cavernous space next to Juantar's Doie Bar that had been converted into an indoor display area for recreational vehicles.

"That's Bohannon's RV Rendezvous—campers, renovated buses. That kind of thing."

"Did Willis say anything about checking that out?"

I looked at my makeshift map. I saw what she was getting at. "He said they checked everything out."

"Looking for freezers and lockers."

"That's what he said."

Janine considered the map. "I have an uncle who owns one of those fancy campers. It has a refrigerator that runs on propane. I bet some of them even have freezers. . . ."

"So you can have frozen pizza at Yellowstone," I said.

"I saw frozen Chicken Kiev at the store the other day. You buy it frozen, zingo, and serve it to your lover while mosquitos buzz outside in the Everglades. That's real romance, Mr. Denson. Do you suppose they checked the RVs as well as the freezer in the office refrigerator?"

"It wouldn't hurt to check it out," I said. "How would you like to go with me tomorrow to have a look at the RVs?"

"Sure. That'd be fun."

"Right now, how about let's go to a movie? It's the least I can do after this dinner. I'll even spring for popcorn."

Janine Hallen said yes. She'd like to see a movie. We went to one, a foreign production—a film, not a movie. Bearded, serious-looking men and intense young women murmured softly in the carpeted lobby before the movie started. Drinkers of white wine, I assumed. "Pauline Kael thought it was provocative," a woman said. Her escort said, "John Simon thought it was pure crap." The woman said, "John Simon hates women." The discussion was ended. I suspected Janine and I were in for an awful movie.

When we got seated, I put my hand in Janine's lap; she wrapped herself around my arm, an affectionate lady. John Simon was right: the movie was pretentious and boring. The poor guy in the lobby was going to have to pretend otherwise if he expected to get far with his date.

Janine Hallen and I left halfway through the torture so we could go to my place to drink a little screw-top red and maybe fool around. I told her I had some raw vegetables in the refrigerator.

"Hmmm!" she said. "Raw vegetables make me friendly. Got your two-shooter loaded?"

That was the first time I ever suspected cauliflower of being an aphrodisiac, and it reinforced my conviction that it is a wonderful vegetable—especially if eaten raw.

22 AS SEEN ON TV

The showroom of Buck Bohannon's RV Rendez-vous was the size of a basketball court and crowded with every kind of camper imaginable. There were Winnebagos, Apaches, Itascas, SportsKings, and a half-dozen other names I'd seen on the highway before. There were long ones and short ones, tall ones and squat ones. There were yellow ones and red ones, blue ones and green ones. Chromium-plated exhaust pipes, mudflaps, mirrors, gee-haws, and doo-dads seemed to stick out at every conceivable angle. There were CB radio antennas on most of the rigs and television disks on the fancier ones, so that intrepid RV travelers might camp among Wyoming antelope and not miss reruns of *Little House on the Prairie*.

Janine Hallen and I were met at the door by none other than Buck Bohannon, impresario of the Rendezvous. I knew that because there was an enormous picture of Buck on the wall with wrestlers behind him. "As Seen on TV," the poster said. "Biggest in Seattle!"

Buck was a large, florid man with an enormous paunch, an oily pompadour maybe thirty years out of fashion, and sideburns that were a trifle too long. "Mornin' folks," he said. "Name's Buck. You may have seen me on TV ads if you watch rasslin'." He gestured to the poster with a wave of his hand.

"I've heard a lot about your TV ads, Mr. Bohannon," I said. "It's a pleasure to meet you in person." I could sense Janine watching me in wonderment.

"You folks came to the right place. You and me both know a man can't go on TV and make a lot of promises to people and not keep 'em," Buck said. "No sir. Folks expect the best when you advertise on TV. They got a right. When I say I'll make you the best deal in the Pacific Northwest, by golly I'll do just that. You got my word on it." Buck Bohannon shook my hand solemnly. He shook my hand the way Augustus Poorman had earlier. Just like Poorman, he was a man of the West, a man of his word. "Ma'am," he said to Janine, "we've got kitchens in some of these rigs you just wouldn't believe."

"I bet that's true," Janine said.

"Just what is it you folks'd be interested in?" Buck looked sincere.

"Well, we're not sure," I said. "We're both hard workers and have got a few bucks ahead. We want to get outdoors a little and air our pants out. You know how it is."

Bohannon laughed—a great, booming *haw, haw, haw* of laughter that showed crooked teeth browned from tobacco. He lit up a Winston and inhaled dramatically. "Yes, sir, I do know how that is, believe me. You want to enjoy the great outdoors but you don't want to spend all your time fumbling around with tent poles in a rainstorm or digging sand out of your private parts—begging your pardon, ma'am. There's more and more people feel just the same as you. I tell you what, we've got lists of all kinds of folks who go on caravans with these rigs: rock hounds, camera nuts, fly fishermen; heck, I can even get you in touch with swingers who caravan, if you're of a mind." He winked at me, went *haw, haw, haw* again, and took another drag on his Winston.

"Swingers? Really?" Janine asked.

Bohannon repressed a choke. He hadn't paid much attention to Janine before, but now he regarded her with interest. "Yes, ma'am." He ran his hand over his pompadour. "These are modern times. RV-ers are liberated same as everybody else."

"I'm interested in what you had to say about kitchens," she said.

"Kitchens?" Bohannon seemed confused. He hadn't recovered from Janine's interest in swinging caravaners. "Oh, sure. You want a good kitchen in an RV. You don't want to be a prisoner to hookups, but you want all the comforts—a food processor, a juicer, a good stove. Gotta have a good microwave. Nothing worse than trying to cook a meal over one of them outdoor barbecues. They pick your pocket for green wood."

"Spend all your time eating burnt food," I said.

"Exactly," Bohannon said. "That's exactly it. If you're a boy scout I suppose you don't mind eating scorched weenies."

Janine said, "We want the best."

Bohannon examined the ash of his cigarette. "Ma'am, we ain't got nothing but the best here at Bohannon's. You seen it on TV. You got my word on it. I got RVs with the works—cuisine centers, we call 'em. I tell you something, I got an outfit that's got a patio that pulls out from the side. You can drive that rig right straight into skeeter country, British Columbia, if you want, or Alaska. Skeeters there got beaks like woodpeckers. Old John can sit out there and have himself a martini and watch the bugs being zapped in our special electronic screen. Skeeters come a-cruisin' in on you at maybe eleven o'clock high, and *vvvvt!* Snap! Crackle! Snip! Snap! Fun to watch 'em burn. And you, ma'am." Bohannon scoped the curve of Janine's blue jeans. "You can get some Chun King chop suey outa the freezer and fix him something special. Nothing like a little gourmet food at trail's end." He pronounced it gor-met.

"Yes, I think we'd want a freezer," she said.

"Afterward you can throw the plates and silverware in the dishwasher, and you and old John here can warm things up a little if you want." The TV personality was getting a bit daring. Buck Bohannon rested his hand on his paunch, sucked in some Winston, and glanced at his reflection in a rearview mirror on the side of an RV. He liked what he saw and smiled just a little.

"We'd like to see the ones with the freezers," I said.

Janine said, "We can stock up on TV dinners before we go."

"Sure, sure," Bohannon said. "I like a good TV dinner myself. Don't kid yourself, those people know how to make a meal. I tell you what I'll do, folks, I'll match any deal you can come up with in the Pacific Northwest. Any deal. Look, some outfits have these rigs sitting on a floor for months. When they sell one they have to make some real money in order to pay for overhead. I don't work that way. Like I say on TV, I like to make folks happy. I make a couple of bucks, sure. I have to. But I work on volume. A man makes a couple of bucks each off a whole lot of RVs, why he can make an honest living and a whole lot of people happy at the same time."

"Just like you say on TV," Janine said.

"That's right, ma'am. You can't B.S. people on TV and get away with it. You can't say it on TV if it ain't so. Let me show you folks some outfits." Bohannon strode forth. He hitched up his Levi's by hooking his thumbs in his belt loops. He gave us a running pitch over his shoulder as he headed for an enormous Winnebago. "I'm going to show you a real special 'Bago first; this one's been customized by a shop here in Seattle. Special job. You can latch a boat on top if you want to do a little fishing. You can pop a trail bike on the back so as to get up in the woods. That's in addition to a hitch for your Jeep, if you have one."

"John and I have a small helicopter," Janine said. "We were wondering . . ."

Buck lit another cigarette, thinking fast. "No problem, no problem. A helicopter? I can have mounts in place in twenty-four hours. No problem. Got me a guy here in Seattle who can do anything."

"That's along with the fishing boat, the trail bike, and the Jeep?" she asked. "We like to zoom and roar."

Good thing we were walking behind Bohannon. Janine put a finger up to her lips, a signal for me not to laugh. She was having fun. I was thinking of asking him about the odds of taking along a two-person submarine, but thought better of it.

Buck said, "No problem. Hell, my guy's made ski racks, dune-buggy racks, hang-glider racks. No reason he can't fix something up for a reasonable-sized helicopter. You got Buck Bohannon's word on it."

Janine gave me a nudge. "Also, we are interested in, you know, the list you mentioned." She looked shy. She cleared her throat.

Buck perked up. "The swinging caravaners?"

Janine looked at the floor.

I said, "Well, yes, that and the rest of them. You know, rock hounds, whatever."

"No problem. No problem." Bohannon walked with extra energy. He put a friendly hand on Janine's shoulder when we got to the fabulous 'Bago.

The Winnebago was decked out with enough gear to compete with the U.S.S. *Enterprise*. Buck lost some of his energy when we looked at the kitchen. The propane freezer was missing. He took us to another RV. The freezer was missing from that one also. All told, four propane-operated freezers were missing from Buck's RVs.

"Well, I'll be damned." Buck scratched his head. "Shoplifters! Can you beat that?"

"Can one man carry one of those by himself?" Janine asked.

"Little lady, you could carry one around by yourself if you wanted. There's not much to them other than plastic and insulation. These rigs is made out of them same stuff as the space shuttle. It was NASA technology that made these outfits possible. I bet you seen that on TV."

23 AMANITA MUSCARIA

Janine Hallen and I walked next door to have
lunch at the Doie Bar and consider the question of the missing freezers from Buck Bohannon's RV showroom. We each had a Doie Boig
with Yellow Crud. That meant cheeseburger in
Juantar's lingo, but there was no explanation
of that on the menu. Juantar liked to yell,
"Boig with crud!" to his cook while his customers shook their heads in mock disgust.

I told Juantar I wanted to speak to him alone
with Janine Hallen. Juantar got a goofy look on
his face when I introduced her. Whenever I got
Juantar around polite company, he rose to the
occasion.

Juantar said, "I wouldn't be seen around
Denson if I were you. People will think you're
letting him pork you. Praise Jesus!" Juantar
waggled his eyebrows.

I said, "Calm down, Juantar, and sit."

Juantar sat. "Good taste, Denson. I like blonds
myself. Never had a bad one." He licked his
lips.

"I need a favor."

"I used to go with a blond pretty regular," he said. "She had these great tits." Juantar held his hands in front of his chest to demonstrate. "They were like sucking on persimmons. Mmmmm! Yum!"

I said, "Come on, Juantar, give us a break."

"Begging your pardon, ma'am," he said to Janine. "I generally have a ravenous appetite, given to gluttony. I'll be serious, Denson. I can do it, really, I can."

I said, "Juantar, I want to go through your basement entrance to the underground."

Juantar looked across the street at the pergola. "Cops came by and said be sure not to let people down there. This have to do with the guy being cut up? If the killer would come around here, I'd give him a price for his supply. Doesn't make any difference what kind of meat you use in the chili. The spices cover it up. I'd do it. You know I would."

"It has to do with the goings-on across the street, that's so," I said.

Juantar glanced at Janine, then me. "Leave me your corpses in your will." He took a key from his ring and gave it to me.

"You see Willie lately?"

"He was in here throwing a while ago. He was looking for you. He'll be back. He came in here with his brother, Rodney, and their friend, Prib somebody. Big guy! Looked like one of those sumos." Juantar squared his shoulders and pushed his stomach out.

"Rodney?" Rodney Prettybird lived in Astoria,

Oregon, and on the rare occasions he did get to Seattle, he spent little time with his brother, preferring, Willie said, the company of fishermen. I'd never met him.

"Looks like Willie, only younger, a little wilder, maybe. He's been here throwing darts with Willie and Prib. They aren't bad, Willie says. And where've you been, Brother Denson?" He leered at Janine, grinning.

"Working, Juantar, I can't make a living throwing darts."

Juantar checked his wristwatch. "Willie ought to be back in a few minutes. He said if you came in you should wait."

I told Juantar we'd wait. Twenty minutes later, Willie Prettybird and Prib Ostrow came in, with Willie unfolding the slender wallet-like leather case that held his darts. They were followed by a third man who I knew was Rodney Prettybird. Juantar was right; he looked just like Willie, only younger and tougher; he had what I can only describe as a mellow expression on his Indian features. For that matter, Prib looked pretty much in an up mood.

"Ass Eyes! Where've you been? Janine!" Willie said. He was pleased to see us.

I said, "Looking for you, Chief Dumbshit."

"It's him, by God, the detective. We was talkin' about you, Denson, wasn't we, Willie?" Willie's large companion was happy to see me, too. Ostrow was wearing his work clothes. His jeans and heavy boots were streaked with white stains from mixing lime and cement.

I introduced them to Janine and shook hands with Rodney Prettybird. "The man who gives Doug Egan high blood pressure. Pleased to meet you," I said.

Rodney laughed. "Every once in a while you run across a white guy who's a real asshole, but Egan's the champ. My boats are laid up now, but I don't care. Got my guys scraping hulls. I'm having a great time in Seattle, ain't that right, Prib?" Rodney grinned broadly. "Hell with Astoria."

Rodney's grin was no more euphoric than Prib's. "You said a mouthful, man. You said a mouthful."

"'Course Astoria's got its advantages," Rodney said. He put his arm around his big friend's shoulders. They both looked happy.

They both were on some kind of drug. It was apparently okay for them to drink alcohol because Rodney ordered two large pitchers of Henry Weinhards.

Willie said, "Haven't you got more class than to bring a civilized woman into a place like this, Buttocks Lips?"

"You gotta respect these lips, Chief. They've kissed hundreds of women, beautiful and otherwise, redheads, brunettes . . ." I glanced at Janine. ". . . blonds, even. Twice that number of breasts—from little tungsten-hard numbers to great, flubbery swamps of yuch!"

"Sure, sure," Willie said.

"These lips have eaten raw baby eels in Kyoto, *uitsmiters* in Amsterdam, *jamon serrano* in Seville."

"Peanut butter sandwiches I can believe."

"These lips have told outrageous lies. I once climbed K-2 without an oxygen tank. Bet you didn't know that. From these lips have issued philosophical insights that remain unappreciated: for example, a man who would lie to his friend is a jerk of the worst sort."

Willie laughed. "White man speaketh the truth. Well said, Fart Breath."

Willie Prettybird was true. Had to be. It was hard for me to believe that Willie could call me Buttocks Lips and still lie to me. For him to call me Fart Breath in public was a gesture of friendship that precluded lying. A failure of character of that magnitude was rare. But not impossible.

Rodney Prettybird said, "I want to thank you on behalf of Willie and Prib. The thing is, I know who the asshole is. No sense you guys wasting all your time running around town."

"You do? Who?" I asked. Willie winked at me. The wink said I should ignore Rodney.

"I told Willie I had the guy fingered. Any son of a bitch does something like this to a man's sister, threatens her like this, a guy's got a responsibility to take care of the matter. You know what I mean?"

"Well, I don't know," I said. "You know I read an article in the *Times* about a guy in Kansas or somewhere who kept getting his hardware store ripped off. It was getting so bad he couldn't afford insurance. The burglar was driving him bankrupt. So he rigged a trip wire across the door and hooked it up to a shotgun. The burglar broke in again, triggered the shotgun, and got his leg blown off. The burglar sued the store owner and won the case—got something nuts, three hundred thousand dollars, I think it was."

Rodney looked beatific. "I'm gonna get the fucker!"

Prib giggled. "Damn right!" he said.

I said, "The thing to do is turn him over to the cops. They've got laws against that kind of thing. See his ass behind bars."

Janine said, "John's right, Rodney."

"Cops!" Rodney said.

"Pah!" Prib muttered.

Rodney said, "Bars, my ass! Sure, they'll maybe send the little whoopie-goo to jail. Give the little sweetcake a couple months." Rodney's voice turned sweet. He made little kissing sounds with his lips much as Willie had made when we learned of the coming of Le Cuisine de Pacifique. "Pat his little heinie! He says he's oh so sorry and promises not to do it again."

Prib said, "Ha!"

"Give his cock a real good twist." Rodney looked happy.

"Lift him right off his feet and make him squeal like a stuck pig, Rodney says. Wee! Wee! Wee!" Looking at Prib, you'd have thought

Prib had gotten a second helping of mashed potatoes. He glowed.

"I'll beat your ass in cricket," Rodney said to Prib.

"Bullshit!" Prib got up to get Juantar's bar darts.

When Prib and Rodney were at the dartboard and out of earshot, I asked Willie what they had been taking.

Willie looked chagrined. "The Latin name is *Amanita muscaria;* it's a mushroom that's all up and down the coast this time of year. Nutty stuff."

Janine was interested. "*Amanita muscaria?*"

"The common name is Fly Agaric—that's either because you can mash it up and put it in milk to kill flies, or because the ancients once associated flies with madness. Nobody knows. The *muscaria* part of the name refers to muscarine, a nerve poison. They contain it in small amounts. There are Siberians who routinely get high off them but the Soviets don't like the idea and want them to drink vodka instead. Northwest Indians used these things in religious ceremonies, but I didn't really know anything about them until Melinda married Mike Stark. You learn a lot about mushrooms being around Mike, I'll say that. He's a shroom freak."

"What kind of ceremonies?" Janine asked.

"There have been all kinds, not only here but in Europe. For example, there's evidence that the plant god Soma worshipped by the Aryans about 2000 B.C. was the Fly Agaric. Only the priests got to eat the shrooms. Everybody else got high drinking the priests' pee."

"Probably'd taste better than beer," I said.

"At Plaincourault, France, there is a Romanesque fresco in an abbey that apparently depicts the Fly Agaric as the Tree of Knowledge."

Janine said, "Have you ever eaten one?"

"Oh, yeah. I tried it out. It made me queasy at first then I felt elated, perfectly wonderful. Then I went to sleep. My girlfriend vomited then felt euphoric. You can eat too many though. An Italian diplomat ate two dozen of them for breakfast in 1893 and it killed him. A lot of people think the Vikings and the ferocious Berserks worked themselves into a murderous frenzy by eating it."

She said, "Muscarine is what does it, then."

"Well, it turns out that muscarine is not the principal poison in Fly Agaric. That honor goes to something called ibotenic acid and muscimol, which are similar."

"What do the mushrooms look like?" I asked.

"They're gorgeous, Denson. Stunners. Their caps range in color from a reddish-orange to a bright, shocking scarlet, as red as a hooker's fingernails. Their stems are an unbelievable virgin white with a skirt. Those red caps have white specks on them. The red shines. You can see your reflection in the red."

"That's what they've been eating." I looked at Rodney and Prib throwing darts.

"I think Rodney brought a few up with him

from Astoria. He dries 'em. They'll be okay as long as Rodney was careful when he picked them and didn't get the idea of trying some *Amanita pantherinas*."

"What would happen then?"

Willie laughed. "They have the same poisons as Fly Agaric, only more of 'em. Rodney's got more sense than that, though. Also I don't think we should pay any attention to his story about knowing who the thug is. I think that's so much talk."

I saw that Rodney and Prib were starting another game. "Willie, a cop told me that one of the guys who got beaten up for being in bed with Melinda was Kim Hartwig, Moby Rappaport's law clerk."

Willie looked chagrined. "I know. I know."

"Hartwig was reported missing the same time as Rappaport. Why didn't you tell me he was one of the victims of Melinda's tormentor? Why, Willie?"

Willie refilled his glass from the pitcher. "Melinda asked me not to."

"Oh, for Christ's sake, Willie, I asked you to tell me the whole truth. Why didn't she want you to tell me?"

"She said people would jump to the conclusion she was sleeping with him to get information about the Cowlitz lawsuit and no good would be served. She said she knew she shouldn't get involved with him but she couldn't help herself."

"And you went along with it?"

"She's my sister, Denson. His being Rappaport's clerk doesn't have anything to do with the other guys getting beaten up. Melinda does not lie to me. She doesn't."

"I just don't know, Chief. Look at it from my point of view. How would you feel? What would you think?"

Willie slumped in the booth.

"I've got another question. Why didn't you tell me you and Rodney had tried to buy the SalPacInc cannery? Foxx Jensen's your opposition in that. In order to check out people with motives I have to know who they are."

Willie said, "Yes, yes." He was miserable.

"You knew I had that Hillendale's job. You knew I was going over to that cannery. And yet you didn't say anything? Janine and I have a right to some straight answers, Willie."

"Denson, you have to believe me: I just didn't think it was relevant. I don't talk about moves like that because if the wrong people find out, it can cost me money. We've got a bundle riding on the line. Who needs to blow a lot of bucks through loose talk? We're talking about thugs beating up Melinda's boyfriends, not our bidding for a cannery."

"We can't help you out unless you tell us the truth—the whole truth, Willie."

"Don't call me Willie. Call me Chief Dumbshit."

I sighed. Try as I might, I couldn't suspect Willie Prettybird of committing any kind of crime. He didn't have it in him. He was my friend. "Okay, Chief Dumbshit it is," I said. "Man you sure act like it sometimes."

Willie Prettybird grinned, "Master of Zen Darts, my ass."

Just then Juantar came jaggle-jooging along, doing little herky-jerky steps. "Friends! Friends! Praise Jesus! Praise the Lord!" He waggled his eyebrows salaciously. "Madame, how are you holding up over here all alone?" His wrists went limp. "With all these hunks," he lisped, and blew us two kisses. "How's your dart, Big Boy?" he asked Willie, who was playing with his dart case.

I didn't hear Willie's reply. I wondered just who had set me up with the man who claimed to be a Hillendale's buyer—Foxx Jensen or Willie Prettybird. The odds were that it was Jensen, still . . .

Juantar said, "Let us consult the Holy Book of truth for the truth shall set us free. Praise God! Yes, it shall. Yes, it shall. Set us free. That's what we are told. Isn't that rich? Isn't that wonderful? We'll all be saved, Praise God, and the truth shall set us free." Juantar gestured toward the pergola across the street. "I wonder if that dead gentleman across the street knew the truth? Did he, I wonder? Did he? Do you reckon, friends, he would have been better off knowing the truth?" Juantar pulled on his ear and wiggled it and went hee, hee, hee. Oh, the mirth, the gesture said.

24 PARTICLES OF CLAY, TRAINED DOGS

The pall of melancholy about Richard Willis was so heavy that even in his vested, bow-tied outfit—which ordinarily would have made a bookie blush—he had about him the air of an undertaker. He ordinarily looked as sharp as the crease on his trousers. He looked rumpled now. He glowered. He pursed his mouth. His lips whitened. He let me wait opposite his desk. I didn't mind. I understood the reasons behind his depression. He wondered how far he should go in his agreement with me. He felt pushed, pressed. He had little choice but to work with me.

Richard Willis's only chance to rescue his career was to catch the butcher before his tormentors did. "Close the door, will you, Denson. The bastards around this place have ears everywhere. We have to talk."

I closed the door. "That's why I work alone," I said. "It costs me more for medical insurance and I have to invest in my own retirement fund, but I don't have to endure what you're going through."

"I talked to Harner for you."

"What'd he say?"

"Something interesting."

"Well?"

Willis shook his head sadly. "You know, Denson, it's a good thing you're a forthright kind of guy. You could get yourself in trouble. This is a perfect example of why we're a trifle cool on private investigators around here." Willis looked malicious, then thoughtful. He was having fun tormenting me. We were partners now, and partners tormented one another. "On the other hand, a little jail might do a guy like you some good. You ever stop to think of that?"

"Oh, for God's sakes. I told Harner everything I know."

"Level with me, Denson, just how many loud-voiced little Southerners do you know who work for Hillendale's and walk around wearing a white cowboy hat and fancy black gloves? Be honest, now. I'm curious."

"If he'd come wearing a three-piece suit and talking about drinking cauwfie and driving cahs, I'd have been more careful. He was just too odd not to be true."

"He waved an easy buck in front of your face."

"Well, there's that, too." I dug my wallet out of my hip pocket and gave Willis the card on which I had scrawled the number of the

Hillendale's employee I'd talked to. "You call this woman and see if she doesn't remember an odd call from a private detective. It was a call from Seattle, Washington. How could she forget? To a New Yorker, living in Seattle is like living on Pluto or Saturn. So what is it? I was set up without even knowing it. Is that it? I'm Willie's friend, blame me, blame him. Let me tell you there're a few people out there who don't like the Prettybirds."

"Like maybe Foxx Jensen?" Willis asked.

"He's one."

"The Prettybirds sell salmon to that cannery. As a matter of fact they've been trying to buy it. You're a friend of Willie Prettybird's. Did you know somebody's been fucking around with the machinery in Jim's cannery?"

"Davis mentioned they'd been having trouble when we were there."

"Denson, the reservation cops and the FBI were watching you every second you were in that cannery. Davis was working with them." Willis pulled a photograph out of an envelope and showed it to me. "Is this the guy?"

It was Augustus Poorman. "My ol' pardner," I said.

"His real name is Ross Trumble. He's a con man with a rap sheet a yard long. He's a friend of Foxx Jensen's too; Harner's got the two of them on tape making all kinds of fun little bargains."

"Well, now!"

Willis opened a roll of Tums. "Yes, sir!

You've got that right. Do you know what Poorman did while you were standing there at that canning line thinking about how you were going to spend your Hillendale's check?"

"No idea."

"He was lacing those open cans with botulism, that's what he was doing."

What could I say. "Oops!"

"Lucky for you Davis let Harner know when you called for the appointment, so Harner and the FBI had people watching the action. You were clear, no problem."

"A little trashing to bring down Jim Davis's asking price. The only problem is if the Foxx brings down Davis's asking price, he brings it down for the Prettybirds too."

"Sure, unless he's able to blame the trashing on Willie and Rodney Prettybird," Willis said.

"I'm Willie's friend. Hook me into accompanying Poorman, Willie gets blamed."

"Poorman scoots on back to Houston, where he's from. That's how Dan Harner sees it. You're talking about some heavy-duty charges. Extortion, for one. He was risking a murder rap with that botulism."

"Ol' Fox loves his dog. Maybe that'll help him out in court. Strikes me that a man willing to poison people to discredit the Prettybirds just might be willing to kill a judge and blame that on them too. You never know. Parts of the body show up in the shadow of the totem pole in Pioneer Place."

Willis said, "The thought had occurred to

me, I'll admit. Incidentally, we might have some charges coming down on Egan too."

"Screwing around with justice."

"The lawyers have big fancy words for it, Denson. I don't know if any of this has anything to do with Rappaport being chopped up or not. With this kid Hartwig missing, I don't think we're looking at the psycho."

"I agree," I said.

"Somebody who hates judges or courts."

"That's the best bet."

"Could be this salmon business. Could be something else—another one of Rappaport's decisions."

"Anything's possible," I said.

"For the present, there's not much I can do except work the nut lists—maybe I can find one who appeared in Rappaport's court, something like that. I have to sneak into records late at night and do my work in secret like some damn thief. The problem with psychos, Denson, is that they can lay dormant for years, like Mt. St. Helens, or what's worse, you don't know who they are. They haven't been identified. You can be talking to an apparently sane person who's in fact crazier than a loon." Willis shook his head.

"Everybody is crazy except me and thee, and sometimes I suspect even thee might be a little touched," I said.

"That's exactly it."

"For all I know you like to wear women's underwear."

Willis glowered.

I said, "You must have some kind of lab analysis of the physical evidence by now. Surely that's allowed."

"The tech people said the flesh has been kept in a freezer, not on ice. They found traces of fired clay on the grain of the cuts."

"Brick dust?"

"That's the best guess. It could be something else. An analysis of the cut flesh suggests that the cutting blade is broad-gauged and ragged—apparently not a hacksaw or meat cutting blade."

"A brick saw then."

"A brick saw or chainsaw. The lab people say a clean steel blade with conventional teeth wouldn't collect that much residue. There were more clay particles in the earliest pieces—the chunk of ankle and the slice of thigh. It could be a brick saw or it could have been a chainsaw that had been allowed to lie in the back of a pickup in which the accumulation of dust might account for the clay. Either alternative is plausible, the lab people say. There were fewer particles beginning with the hunk of forearm. The body was cut into large chunks first, then frozen."

"If the tech people can say all that about the saw, why can't they identify the body?"

"It's blood type O. A middle-aged man. I think they've got him I.D.'d but aren't saying anything."

"Rappaport?"

"There are people here in the department who would make book on it," Willis said.

"The lab people think the blade got cleaner with every slice of frozen flesh, is that it?"

"That's their best guess. Do you know of any brickmasons associated with this case?"

I couldn't think of any. I started to say no, but stopped. I remembered Prib, Willie's friend. He was a bricklayer. He'd had lime stains on his clothes at the Doie. I thought of Willie. Both Janine and I thought he was telling the truth. in the Doie. "I know one," I said.

"You do? Who?"

I told him about Prib Ostrow.

"He look psycho to you?"

"Oh, I wouldn't think so. He's large and full of energy. Devoted to the Prettybirds, but I don't think he's nuts."

"You never know about psychos, Denson. I'll check to see if Ostrow has any kind of record. You know, all these doo-dahs think they have to do is wait. He'll keep rationing the pieces away until he runs out of corpse or gets caught."

"What happens if he uses up Rappaport's corpse and they still haven't caught him?"

Willis said, "Then maybe he finds himself another judge to kill. And maybe another law clerk, too. We've still got that to consider."

"The only thing is that if Prib Ostrow is involved . . ." I waited for Richard Willis to finish the sentence.

Willis didn't hesitate. ". . . then we're probably looking at the Prettybirds."

The logic was inescapable. "At Willie," I
said.

"Yes, we are. Or Rodney."

"Willie Prettybird didn't have anything to do
with freezing a man and cutting him up with a
brick saw. If you're around a person long
enough you get to know what somebody can
and can't do."

"Oh, you know that's bullshit." Willis was
disgusted with me. "Gut feelings don't count.
You can never know what's going on inside
somebody's mind, not really. Only facts count."

I told him about the visit Janine Hallen and
I had made to Buck Bohannon's RV Rendezvous.

Richard Willis pulled a sheet of paper out of
his jacket. He put on a pair of reading glasses.
He read the paper through. He looked at me
and adjusted his glasses. He reread it. Finally
he said, "Some of the guys on this force,
Denson—and some of them we make detectives
so as not to be accused of discriminating
against stupidity—are so damn dumb they
can't pour piss out of a boot with the directions written on the heel."

"I bet they didn't check the RVs for freezers."

Willis was infuriated with his colleagues. He
said nothing. His silence was his answer.

"See. There you go. Here you are, complain-
ing about a computer," I said. "At least Toba
does what it's told."

"I want you to watch the Prettybirds and

Prib Ostrow. If the cops around here want to spend their time choking their chickens, let them."

"Harner didn't seem like a bad guy."

"Dan's okay," Willis said. "He's lucky he's got a broken ankle—gives him a chance to stand clear of this butcher murder debacle."

"Maybe you're lucky, too."

Willis grinned. "Yes, maybe I am."

"Any new ideas on how the murderer is smuggling those chunks past cameras? That's a curious one, I have to admit. Under the circumstances, Toba should have done the job."

Willis took another drink of whiskey. "Judging from the scuttlebutt in the cafeteria, they've thought of everything from trained dogs to catapults. A guy who trains dogs for the Army at Fort Lewis said a smart dog could do it. The iron fence is too short to stop a strong dog. Give him the right dog, he said. With all the mongrels that hang out at that place, just how in the hell are we going to catch a guy with a trained dog, Denson? Do you want to tell me that?" Willis had to beat the department. Had to. The trained dog possibility was a complication Willis didn't like. His face tightened.

All I could think about was a smart German shorthair who'd once cleared a barbed-wire fence in pursuit of a goose. Was big George running errands for Foxx Jensen in exchange for a nuzzle behind the ears and a little extra liver?

25 A HOWLING

The door to the Doie's exit to the Seattle underground was at least fifty years old, so I really didn't need a key to go through it. There were so many tiny cracks on the black enamel of the knob that I thought at first it was covered with a cobweb. The key was one of those round old things that are so inefficient they hardly qualify for the name. The flashlight that I had dug out of the trunk of my Fiat went out momentarily, so I whacked it on the side of my leg. The battery was a couple of years old and didn't have a whole lot of poop left.

I turned to Janine and said, "One thing an experienced detective does is check out his equipment before he goes on an assignment."

"I see I'm in good hands, Mr. Denson: you bring one flashlight that doesn't work for two people to share."

I trained the yellow light on the hole and inserted the key Juantar had given me.

Behind me, Janine Hallen said, "A bright light'd probably hurt our eyes anyway."

"There's one thing I should warn you about."

"What's . . ." Janine suddenly gagged and started spitting.

"Check for cobwebs before you start to talk."

"A person feels real safe with you."

I checked the corroded door hinges but couldn't tell in the poor light whether they'd been used recently. I turned the key and pushed on the door, which didn't want to move at first. "After you, ma'am."

"No, no you first, Mr. Denson. I know you're a gentleman. You go on ahead."

I waved my hand in front of me to catch any cobs that might have been strung down by the open door. I stepped onto the floor of the underground passageway directly underneath the sidewalk along Yesler Way. The air smelled like a week-old wet towel. I squatted, and when I put my hand out for balance I touched warmth.

Something raced up my shoulder, brushed against my face.

I jerked back.

My head cracked into Janine's face. "Ouch!" she said.

"A fucking rat! Yyyaaagggh!" I was disgusted to the point of feeling sick. A rat!

Janine spit in the blackness. "Got me in the mouth with your head."

"Are you still with me?"

"You've got a hard head, but I'm okay."

I trained the yellow light on the map. Janine and I had had to estimate the length of the sidewalk in front of Juantar's Doie Bar and Buck Bohannon's RV Rendezvous next door. "I'll put my beam on the floor. You watch the base of the buildings." I stepped forward slowly with Janine Hallen's left hand holding onto the collar of my jacket.

We had gone about fifteen yards when she said softly, "I think this must be the common wall, John."

She was right. We were at the place where a brick wall separated the Doie from the Rendezvous.

I turned out my light. "If this screwball happens to catch us down here, I'll douse the light," I whispered. "Don't move. We'll let him move around if he wants, but we stay still."

"We stay still," Janine whispered.

I can be nonsexist only up to a point. "You let me take care of him."

"Sure. I saw you handle the rat, remember?"

"Listen, James Bond couldn't have handled that rat any better," I said.

"James Bond wouldn't have mashed my lip."

I gave her a gentle elbow. I turned my flashlight on again and whacked it against my leg. We continued slowly down the underground sidewalk in front of Buck Bohannon's RV Rendezvous.

We continued until Janine said, "Door."

"Ahh," I said. I tried Juantar's key in the decrepit lock. It didn't fit. I tried my handy-dandy lock pick. It didn't work.

"Very smooth there, James."

I tried the pick again. The door opened. It was easier than the one below the Doie. "You give up too easily." We entered Buck Bohannon's basement. I closed the door and doused my flashlight again.

"I bet even I could get through a lock that old," she said.

"Not a bad point. All the killer had to do was slip downstairs at the Doie, pop the lock of Juantar's door and this one, and he was inside Buck's. Easy to lug those RV freezers down here. But then where?" Janine was so close to me I could smell her. The aroma was lovely. There is no odor so grand as that of a woman who likes you and wants to go to bed with you. I led Janine back to the underground sidewalk and relocked the door to Buck's basement. I shined my light up at the metal support beneath the sidewalk above.

I started back toward the door to Juantar's bar with Janine's hand at my collar.

"Did you ever see *The Thing* when you were a kid?" she asked.

"I know. I know. This is spooky."

She stopped suddenly. "Hear that?"

I'd heard it. A sound farther down the sidewalk beneath the sidewalk. "Another rat, I think."

Janine said, "I almost peed in my pants when I saw that movie. Had nightmares for weeks. Do you think we're onto something?"

"I think the killer probably stole those freezers from Buck."

"To store the corpse."

"I don't think he's using them to make ice cubes."

"How is he ..." Janine gripped my collar a tad bit tighter. "... you know, doing that to the body?"

"How is he cutting up the corpse? Willis's lab boys say they're being sawed after they were frozen. They think he's using a brick saw or a chainsaw."

"From which you deduce?"

"We're looking for a psychopath who owns a brick saw or a chainsaw."

"Cutting a frozen corpse into steaks and chops. Brrrr! I think I have to go to the bathroom."

"Gonna wet 'em again, eh? A cool lady lawyer like you, afraid of a little screwball."

I opened the door into the Doie and was about to step inside when I heard it—we both heard it: a low, mournful howling, that rose, wavered momentarily, then faded.

"What's that?" Janine asked.

"Don't know," I said.

We heard some yips and yelps, then the howling again, stronger this time, a howling that rose and fell, rose and fell. The howling stopped. We heard two discontented barks. Then nothing.

"A dog," she said.

"No, no. That's a coyote. I grew up in a place called Cayuse, Oregon. I heard them all the time."

"A coyote?"

"Or maybe a human doing an imitation of a coyote." We listened for more howling, but there was none. Then again maybe she was right, I thought. Maybe it was a dog. I whistled loudly twice. "Hey, George! Come here, boy. Come here." I whistled three more times. "George!" I called.

There was no answer. The Seattle underground was quiet.

At last, Janine said, "Scoot. Let's get out of here."

I didn't need a whole lot of persuading. The business about the coyote or dog, though, I found interesting. "Do you think a miniature German shorthair could make a racket like that?" I asked.

"As a matter of fact, my cousin Bobby owned one. Sure it could."

We both giggled with relief when we were upstairs sitting safely in one of the Doie's booths. Juantar saw us and came over, giggling, rubbing his hands together. "Praise Jesus, you two do look pale. How about some hot spiced wine? You'll like it, Denson, it's made with screw-top and some extra goo. It'll put some color in your cheeks. Praise the Lord!"

"Put something strong in it, Juantar. Some brandy or something. How about some vodka?"

"I can go pee-pee in it if you want," Juantar drawled.

"A little booze'll do, thanks, Juantar."

"Praise God!" Juantar stroked his curly beard. He went to get the wine.

Janine's lower lip was swollen and split slightly on one side. She touched it with the tips of her fingers. "If my lip's out of commission you've got only yourself to blame."

Juantar spotted the swollen lip when he returned with the drinks. "My, my, a passionate couple." Juantar leered at me. "Oh, you big boy, you."

"Go, Juantar," I said.

Juantar went, saying, "Praise the Lord. Praise Jesus!" Juantar didn't count a whole lot on the Christian trade.

Janine felt her lip again. "So where is he hiding the freezers, John? The underground?" This was the first time she had tried the detective business and she was excited. She had a quick mind.

"A while back the city hired some engineers to shore up the supports under the sidewalks. To do that they'd've had to map the entire underground. The cops knew what was down there when they searched it. Nothing, Willis said."

"The killer wouldn't need much space," she said. "Engineers are human. They make mistakes. In the middle of the night he'd be alone down there."

She was right, of course. Engineers, cops, and private investigators are all human. "What do you think we should do?"

"For starters, I think one of us should do a

little library work. Me. I've spent half my life in a library. Point me in the right direction; I know how to find things."

"It's worth a try. If you haven't already, you might take one of those tours to get a feel for the place."

"I went with some friends once. Poe would have loved it down there. I'll trace the underground back as far as I can, then start from what's known of the beginning and work forward," Janine said.

"Looking for what?"

"Variations in the original plan of the underground. A bunch of high school kids cleaned this place up in the late 1960s—maybe they overlooked something. Maybe the engineers overlooked something."

26 WILLIS GOES UNDERGROUND

Richard Willis could not understand why I would willingly choose to hang out at Juantar's Doie Bar. He surveyed the Doie with a look of amazement on his face. Two women played cribbage. A man worked a crossword puzzle. Juantar strode back and forth behind the bar talking to an old man in a small hat. Juantar motioned crazily with his hands as he talked. He gestured to the bullet-ridden silhouettes behind the bar, talking all the while.

"Guys like you are beyond me, Denson," he said. "On the face of it you're a bright enough guy, yet you willingly choose to hang out in a place like this. What a collection of creeps!"

I'd told Willis to dress casually, but there he was with a spiffy jacket and bow tie. I said, "You look like a waiter in a bus station."

"Like a what?"

"I like your tie. Is that one of those clip-on things or what?" I asked. I flipped the end of his tie with my finger.

"A clip-on tie?" Willis's face tightened, then he relaxed. "Denson, if I didn't have my career on the line . . ."

"I had clip-ons in high school," I said cheerfully. "Nobody in my family knew how to tie ties. My old man worked with his hands. I also had a crewcut that I rubbed alum on so the hair stuck straight up like hard little spikes. Really, if you're the kind of guy who wears ties, I'd think clip-ons would be just the thing. You just slide 'em on your collar there, and bingo! You've got that executive look, a professional." I started to lift Willis's collar but he drew his head back.

Willis made a curious sound in his throat, half rumble, half growl. He had made a decision to accept me, a private detective, responsible to very little that he could see—a flake on the make for an easy laugh.

Juantar Chauvin saw us and came over, going through one of his hippity-hop routines like an overgrown, bearded rabbit. He waggled his eyebrows. He gave Willis one of the Doie's whorehouse tokens—his gift to new customers.

Willis read it and burst out laughing.

"Everybody in here likes to doie," Juantar said. "You're the first bow-tied man we've had, the very first. Is this an occasion? Are you some kind of preacher?" He looked at me. "Are you born again, Denson? Praise Jesus!"

"We're going underground tonight, Juantar," I said.

"Down there?" Juantar motioned toward the floor with his forehead. "Denson, Denson, there could be a boogie down there butchering people. Steady customers are hard to come by. I

value my portion of your income." He whistled
a little riff. "What can I get you?"

"We'll each take a double whiskey," Willis
said.

Juantar said, "The man on the tube news
said they found a rump roast across the street
last night. Belongs to a younger man." He
made a loud sucking sound, *wzzzpt*, and looked
salacious. "Oh, Sodom! Sodom!" Juantar headed
for the bar to get our drinks and change the
reggae tape.

Willis stared after Juantar. "Jesus Christ!"

"Could the younger man be Kim Hartwig?" I
asked.

"I'd bet on it. Frozen solid and packed away
in an RV freezer like the good judge."

When Juantar got back with our drinks, he
asked Willis whether or not it was illegal to
run an ad in the *Times* and *P.I.* saying people
could drink beer at the Doie and watch meat
deliveries at the pergola across the street.

A half-hour later, Richard Willis and I eased
open the door in the Doie's basement and
stepped onto the underground sidewalk. I had
a new flashlight but wished I hadn't drunk the
whiskey. Aside from a beer or a little screw-top
red, I'm not much of a drinker. Whenever I
drink distilled liquor, gnomes hop up and
down on my brain with their feet.

"Turn that fucking thing out," Willis whispered.

I turned my light out, remembering the rat
that had run up my arm the night before.
"There're rats down here."

"A rat now and then's good for you. Right now we've got a psychopath on our hands."

We squatted there, listening. We heard a rustle down the sidewalk in the direction of First Avenue.

"Rat," I said. "Didn't I tell you?"

I heard a muffled yipping. "What's that?"

One more yip.

"The coyote!"

"Shhhh!" Willis shushed me quiet.

"It wasn't a rat."

"I said shhh."

I stayed shushed until the sound was gone. "There're underground sidewalks on both sides of the street. That's not to mention all the abandoned underground businesses. He could be anywhere. He's got all night."

"You may be right about that." Willis started walking slowly in the direction of the sound we had heard, feeling the block wall of the street side as he went.

I followed, saying nothing. My stomach rumbled loudly, beginning with a high-pitched *weemie-weemie* sound that ended with a mournful, gurgling lament. I hoped it would stop but it didn't. *Weemie-weemie, gurgle-gurgle*; it got louder. A detective was supposed to be stoic and silent on a job like this. "I had onions on my cheeseburger. I am handy though. I've had girlfriends say I have quick hands."

Willis sighed in the darkness. "I bet," he said.

"We need more people to do this. Somebody

for the other side of the street. Three teams if
we could get them, two at a minimum."

Willis wasn't going to save his hide by
running to his colleagues for help. He wanted
to do this by himself. "Just who do you think
we should get?"

"Well, Janine Hallen for starters." I heard
another sound up ahead.

"Hear that?" Willis whispered.

"I heard it."

"A rat this time," he said.

"Janine's smarter than hell. She's got a cool
head."

"You can do without getting in her pants for
a couple of nights, Denson. Quit thinking
through your pecker."

"If the killer is down here, he could either be
on the east or west side of First Avenue or the
north or south side of Yesler Way. You have to
go above ground to cross over, so we wouldn't
be able to hear his brick saw if we're on the
wrong side."

Willis knew I was right. "Okay, what're you
thinking?"

"Janine Hallen and me, one team. Humor
me. Juantar Chauvin and you, the second team.
We can figure out some kind of systematic
sweep."

Willis muttered, "Shit," in the darkness.

"Two of us down here chasing rats is stupid,
and you know it."

"Who is Juantar Chauvin?"

I waited for my stomach to finish gurgling

again. "The guy up there who owns the Doie."
I had an idea that wasn't going to go over well.

"What?" Richard Willis almost broke his
professional whisper. "That fool . . ."

"Used to be a lawyer before he got fed up
with dealing with guys like you."

"In a pig's ass. Is that true, Denson?"

"Praise Jesus!" I mimicked Juantar's Bayou
drawl.

Richard Willis fell into a stubborn silence.
He didn't want to give up on catching the
butcher by himself; this was important to his
dream of vindication, of giving a big raspberry
to the department suck-butts, of surviving the
departmental effort at busting a cop whose
standards were too high to include everybody.
Janine and Juantar were the only two people I
could think of. I certainly couldn't go to Willie
Prettybird or his friend Prib Ostrow.

We sat there in the musty air saying nothing
for more than half an hour. We listened to the
rats, to our breathing, to my stomach gurgling.
There were occasional footsteps on the ground-
level sidewalk above us—a few drunks, a solo
traveler, Juantar's customers going to and from
the Doie. We heard several couples stop in
front of the huge window that was the sidewalk side of Buck Bohannon's brightly lit RV
showroom.

I was the first one to break the silence. "I
know what this means to you. It'll be your
show, Richard. Your nab. Janine is already
drawing maps showing how this place evolved.

If there's been an unrecorded change made or something overlooked, she'll find it. She's smart as hell, I tell you."

"That's different than stalking a psychopath in this damn maze. There's nobody down here except him and us."

"She's a careful, intelligent woman. I'm sure she can take care of herself. We'll give her a weapon?"

Willis sucked air in between his teeth. "What kind of piece do you carry, Denson?"

"I don't."

"You what?" Willis nearly broke his whisper.

"Can't see the point in it. I'm essentially chickenshit in the presence of violent people. Don't like to be around 'em. I'm fast, though. I've been told that. Chickenshit to the core and faster than a dose of Epsom salts."

"I bet you are."

"I think Janine should carry something though."

"It's your hide."

"You don't need to worry about me," I said. "You know, the motor on a brick saw makes a lot of noise, and Bill Speidel runs tours down here all day long. That means the butcher has to work at night, around Speidel's tours."

Willis agreed. "I can work the psycho angle in the mornings and take naps in the afternoons. I'm supposed to show up at the office but I don't have anything to do. No problem taking a good nap in the afternoon."

"I think that's the way to go."

"Do you think your Praise Jesus friend can stop giggling long enough to help us out?"

"Juantar's not crazy or anything like that, you know. He's just too smart not to recognize the insanity everywhere. He knows it's the small pleasures that count."

"And you're pretty much the same, huh, Denson?"

"Pretty much," I said. I was the opposite in temperament of Richard Willis, but I liked him. He was tidy and orderly, the responsible firstborn. I was loose, intuitive. But Willis was intelligent, give him that. He had integrity. He was an honest man. "The thing we have in common, Willis, is that we don't fit very well in organizations. Your expectations are too high, so they're trying to get rid of you. I don't have any at all, so I quit. Put me in a meeting and I start giggling like Juantar."

"Dammit, Denson, these guys are cops. They're supposed to be professionals."

That set me to giggling. "Supposed to be professionals? Come on. What are you talking about, Willis? My man! My man! You're talking about the Seattle Police Department. The larger the circus, the more curious the show. Everybody knows that. You're pissed off because there're too many clowns who aren't funny. The thing to do is shuck all that."

"No, no, Denson. You got it wrong. I'm a professional cop, a good one. I'm pissed off because the clowns wind up in charge. They think they're funny and they're not."

I shut up. Of course the clowns wound up in charge. That was the first rule of John Denson. Most people have to believe in something. No use in arguing with a believer, though. You either believe or you don't.

I didn't know what to believe when the howling started up again. It sounded like a coyote to me—or a damn good imitation of one.

Willis grabbed me by the arm. "There it is again!"

"You're right about that."

"What is it?"

"Sounds like a coyote to me. Maybe a dog."

"A dog of some kind," Willis said. There was a break while Willis blew his nose. "The only thing I can't figure out is what would a dog be doing in the Seattle underground."

We both shut up and listened. If it was a coyote and not a man or dog, it was a coyote out of place. The lonesome, melancholy howling was an anguished supplication to a moon that could not be seen in the musty, rat-infested bowels of the Seattle underground. I had heard howls of coyotes before, when I was a boy in Cayuse, Oregon, on the banks of the Columbia River. I whistled again, as I had the night before. "Here, George. Come here, boy."

The animal in the bowels of the underground howled once more, then fell silent.

27 BUZZING OF A SAW

Cayuse was on the banks of the Columbia—
way out there in desert country. There were no
natural trees in the country around Cayuse;
except for some stunted sagebrush and small
cacti, the land was bare to the edge of the
water. The original settlers had hopes, though,
and there remained an occasional poplar or
locust by a dry stream bed, just as there were
abandoned farmhouses in the most unlikely
locations. I chased lizards when I was a kid,
shot at scorpions with a BB gun, watched for
rattlers sunning by the railroad tracks.

The call of a coyote was always special to
me. I was a reader when I was a kid and knew
about the Coyote stories the Indians told. I
heard coyotes on warm summer evenings yipping and yelping on the desert behind the bluff
that rose from the Columbia. They gathered in
groups up there and held mysterious, feral
concerts. They yipped and yapped, shadows in
the light of a yellow moon, calling to one
another and petitioning the stars. I saw them
at dusk one night, silhouettes on a distant

223

ridge. They turned their throats to the stars when they howled.

The howls also came from the barren Horse Heaven Hills across the Columbia. The barks came small across the water. The howling was dim as well, almost subliminal, as I listened to it in bed at night. In the winter the howling was a spooky presence behind the noise of the electric heater on the sleeping porch that served as my bedroom. When I was a kid, I believed in Coyote with a capital C every bit as much as some people believe in Jesus or the prophet Muhammad. The only difference was that Coyote talked to me at night, reminded me of his restless presence.

Richard Willis sat beside me, silent by agreement, his impatience momentarily corked while I gave Juantar Chauvin the details of our problem and the nature of our request.

Juantar Chauvin waggled his eyebrows, inflated his cheeks, and whistled a phrase out of "Entrance of the Gladiators," the familiar circus song associated with steam calliopes. "Gentlemen! Gentlemen!" he called, imitating a ringmaster. Then he dropped his voice almost to a whisper, a dramatic trick he'd learned from listening to evangelical preachers. "Y'all're nuttier than a fruitcake if you expect me to go down there at night with a loon on the loose." He drew his head back and appraised each of us in turn. "Praise Jesus, how dumb do you think I am? No, no, no. I'm a barkeep, Denson, I've got customers to entertain."

I said, "Juantar, you got tired of being a lawyer, right? Why was that?"

"Boooaaarrriiinnnggg!" Juantar said. He held his nose between the thumb and forefinger of his left hand.

"So you quit."

"I like to doie, Denson. You know that." Juantar stood and did a little dance.

"Well, this isn't lookie and this isn't feelie. Sometimes you have to get your blood pumping to remind yourself that you're alive."

"But Denson, Denson, there're rats and spiders down there, butcher murderers. You and your friend Dickie the cop here even said there was a coyote or damn dawg down there a-howling and making a racket. That's just too much pumping of blood. Too much." Juantar sighed and did his best to look demented.

For Juantar Chauvin, doie was not just a screw, as on his hooker tokens. For him it meant to act. To know risk. To live. People who were satisfied with lookie and feelie were people who watched television. In Juantar's opinion, the madam who priced the tokens was right: doie was worth five times as much as lookie. I said, "Just as I thought, Juantar, you're all lookie and no doie. We need help."

Juantar looked hurt.

I shook my head. "All lookie. I wouldn't have believed it of you, Juantar. I'm embarrassed for you."

"Dickie the cop'll save me if we meet spookies, won't he? Won't you do that, Dickie?"

"Richard's a professional," I said. "He knows what he's doing."

"There'll be no damn Praise the Lording down there either," Willis said. "We've got a job to do."

"Praise Jesus, I wouldn't do that," Juantar said. He whistled some more circus music. "But what about my Halloween party coming up? I love costumes. I've got folks coming dressed up to frighten people. I do Frighten Your Neighbor on Halloween, Seduce Your Friend on New Year's Eve, and Mardi Gras in February. I've promised prizes. The Doie's reputation is at stake here. What'm ah gonna do?" Juantar turned deliberately Southern on the last sentence.

"Let Tom do it," I said. Tom was Juantar's assistant.

"Well, okay, I'll do it, but you have to buy me a pretend sheriff's badge to pin on my shirt. I've always wanted one of those."

"Done, I'll buy you a badge."

"Can I wear it on my shirt when I'm down there with you, Dickie?"

Willis looked at me, disgusted.

"Doie! Doie! Okay!" Juantar rubbed his hands together.

Juantar Chauvin was going underground with us in pursuit of the butcher murderer.

The first thing on our agenda was a report from Janine, who had researched the underground at the library and had gone on one of Bill Speidel's underground tours.

"Well, from everything I can tell, everything's like it's supposed to be down there," she said. "I don't see anything added or subtracted. The walls and rooms and sidewalks all conform to the maps. There is, however, one possibility we might think about."

"Praise God!" Juantar said.

Willis said, "What is it, Janine?"

"That area was gutted by fire in 1889 and was rebuilt within a few years and still later restored. That's why you have the pergola and the lovely architecture of Occidental Park and Mall. Just after the turn of the century, when the underground was yet flourishing, there was a proposal to dig tunnels through the streets to Pioneer Place Park. The tunnels would meet there and link up the undergrounds of both sides of First Avenue, Yesler Way, and James Street—sort of an early shopping mall. If you hooked the streets up people wouldn't have to go upstairs and cross the street in the rain."

What an idea! "Why didn't they do it?"

"From the newspapers I was able to find, the street-level merchants thought it was a little too good an idea. They were afraid of the competition, and there were more of them than businessmen with shops underground."

"Nobody started digging the tunnels or anything like that, did they?"

Janine said, "There's no mention of it that I could find. They could have, though. An ambitious owner on one side or the other could have closed down for a few weeks and started tunneling. There are months of newspapers that are missing, records that are gone."

"Anything's possible," Willis said.

With that, the four of us sat down to plan our pursuit of the killer. We decided the most likely hours for the butcher murderer to be in his underground hideaway—if our theory was correct—was somewhere between eleven o'clock at night and five in the morning. Juantar would turn the Doie over to his assistant so he could sleep in the daytime and prowl with Willis at night. Willis came up with snub-barreled .38s and shoulder holsters for Juantar and Janine. I carried nothing; I had gotten along without a weapon so far.

It was agreed that Janine and I would start in the south underground of Yesler Way, maybe, or the east underground of First Avenue, then switch with Juantar and Richard Willis—going west or north. With James Street to watch, too, we really needed four or five teams. To get around that problem, Willis asked his police computer to give him a patternless, random rotation that varied both times and directions of our movements. The computer obliged with shift printouts. Willis also came up with two modern versions of the walkie-talkie so we could communicate between streets.

The cops would watch the streets and the pergola with Toba. We would go underground with the rats.

Janine and I drew the south underground sidewalk of Yesler Way our first shift out. We

first went east—away from the pergola. We
didn't talk. We didn't use our flashlights. We
felt our way in the darkness, accepting the
cobwebs and hoping, both of us, that a rat
wouldn't suddenly sprint across a foot or scramble up a leg. When we came to the dead end on
the map Janine had made from her research,
we stopped and squatted, listening to our
breathing. A small beep came on my walkie-
talkie. I punched the button that lit my cheap
digital watch: eleven-thirty. The beep was right
on time. It was Willis, saying he and Juantar
were okay but had found nothing. I gave them
one beep back, as agreed. There would be no
talking on the walkie-talkies unless someone
needed help.

The computer had told us to wait ten minutes before we started west. We waited and the
howling of the coyote began—far, far down the
sidewalk, perhaps around the corner along
First Avenue. It was a dim call, plaintive, clear
for a heartbeat then dim, inhabiting, it seemed,
the realm of the imagination.

I felt Janine's lips against my ear. "Our
friend," she whispered.

I put my lips against her ear. "How far,
would you say?"

I could feel her shrug her shoulders. "The
butcher killer's a psycho. Maybe it's him."

"Maybe it's George," I said.

"Could be."

When our ten minutes were up we started
easing our way to the west again, but when we

approached the corner of Yesler and First Avenue the mournful howling stopped. Our schedule called for a twenty-minute wait at the corner. Two minutes before it was time to beep Juantar and Willis, we heard the call again—in the direction we had come from.

"Hear that?" Janine said.

"I heard it. A man who knew the underground would have had plenty of time to go one level up and circle back. No problem."

"I agree," she said.

"You suppose Foxx Jensen could move George that fast?"

"George is probably pretty quick. Of course, we could be dealing with more than one person."

That was the last time we heard the coyote that shift.

At one o'clock we emerged under the Doie for a cup of coffee and a meeting with Juantar and Willis.

Willis maintained they had heard nothing. "We heard a few rats, that's all. Chauvin here claimed he heard something, but I think it was adrenaline squirting through his brain. I didn't hear anything."

"Brother Willis, Brother Willis, you're wrong. I heard a saw buzzing. I got ears on me. I can hear coons and crawdads kissing in the bayou. We were over there in front of the place where the underground tour ends. I heard a saw."

"Coming from which direction, Juantar?"

"From the west?"

"See what I told you," Willis said. "That's impossible."

"Praise Jesus, I did hear it," Juantar said. "At about twelve-thirty. Tell me you didn't hear the coyote just before we came up, Mr. Policeman. Damn, you're the kind of cop they got in Baton Rouge. Stone deaf. Won't listen to a thing. Won't listen."

"We did hear what sounded like a coyote," Willis said. He didn't want to admit his hearing might be going bad on him. "Somebody's dog on the prowl."

Juantar poured us all more coffee. "Praise Jesus, but that howling was creepy. If it's a dog his owner maybe oughta feed him or something."

"We heard him, too. It's a suffering sound. He's miserable," Janine said.

"He's trying to say something," I said. "He knows we're down there and he's trying to avoid us."

Willis looked at me like I was being ridiculous. "Oh, bullshit, Denson, this isn't a drive-in movie. Use your head. There's an explanation for everything. There's either a nut down here howling like a fucking coyote—excuse me, Janine—or a miserable dog that sounds like a coyote. We find the nut who's doing the howling and we've found a guy with a brick saw and RV freezers full of sawed-up bodies."

"If it's a dog, maybe it's been delivering parts of Moby Rappaport to Pioneer Place. The dog trainer at Fort Lewis said it could be done, didn't he? All you need is a smart, strong dog."

Willis sighed. "All right. Okay. It could be that. It could even be George. Only I think it's a man. A guy who howls is nuts. It'd take a nut to cut people up with a brick saw."

Juantar said, "Maybe we should all take silver stakes with us and a crucifix like in the movies. Praise Jesus! Praise the Lord!"

I said, "The hound of the Bricksawman."

"Sure, sure, that's it," Juantar said. He did a little howling of his own. He turned his curly blond beard to the ceiling and went, "Ah wooooo!"

Richard Willis had by now learned to ignore Juantar. Willis looked at his wristwatch. "The computer says our break's up."

"I did hear a saw a-buzzing," Juantar said. "I did hear one. There's somebody down there cutting up bodies."

"A brick saw or a chainsaw?" I asked.

Juantar said, "Praise Jesus. Could have been either. It's hard to say."

Had Doug Egan gotten the bizarre idea of cutting up Judge Rappaport from watching the chainsaw Rodin carve salmon out of Douglas fir? Anything was possible. Anybody could be a secret psychopath. Both Egan and Jensen had a motive for the murder if they thought Rappaport was about to rule against them.

It was time to go below again and listen to the howling of dogs and the buzzing of saws.

28 ENCOUNTER

Bodily parts were now showing up in Pioneer Place Park once a day, at night always, including fingers, thumbs, toes, ears, and noses, so that the police were forced to acknowledge that they had identified Judge Moby Rappaport and his clerk, Kim Hartwig, as the victims. The admission did not come easily—in fact, the truth was forthcoming only after some vile, unconscionable bastard had tipped off the reporters on the sly. Or so the chief of police said, using various euphemisms and barely repressing his rage. He said he'd only been trying to spare the families of the murdered men.

One does not murder and mutilate the corpses of a judge and his clerk without upsetting the public imagination. There is a hierarchy in the value of human life. One does not murder the child of Charles Lindbergh and have a quiet trial. Homeless drifters are at the other end of the extreme, which is why Juan Corona allegedly murdered one hundred and twenty-six men outside of Fresno before the cops got wise and began unearthing pits of bodies. One should not kill law-abiding family men because that upsets all manner of law-abiding family men. One should not kill cops because that pisses other cops off.

But worst of all, possibly because it strikes at the very heart of everything, is to kill a judge.

The public demanded swift and decisive justice as a deterrent to future butcher killers of judges. The media theater took over, and everybody watched the drama on television or read about it in the *Times* or the *P.I.* Various police officials were put at the top of the playbill. They didn't like it there. The police seemed to dither. Willis's hated police chief, protector of the incompetent cop Willis had slandered in a police meeting, addressed microphones with non sequiturs and tortured logic. The police were held responsible by editorial writers and station managers. The indecisiveness of the police continued. Cops are such dumb shits, people said. Television reporters ran excitedly from public official to public official, woof-woofing like dumb hounds, keeping their quarry excited and hopping about this way and that to provide their photographers with good material.

It was difficult for the reporters to suppress their grins. The chief did his best. He twisted and dodged his way through his tormentors as best he could. He looked, wild-eyed, for the slightest hole in each wounding question.

I suspected that Richard Willis was the source of the department leak about the identity of the corpses. Willis acknowledged it cheerfully as the four of us met for our nightly meeting before going underground.

"Oh, hell, yes," he said. "Serves the dumb bastards right." He smirked. "They know I'm the one who did it, too, but they can't prove it. That's what they get for insisting I hang around the station all day with nothing to do."

"Do you suppose they'll forget it by the time of your disciplinary hearing?"

Willis shook his finger in front of my face. "Listen here, those guys gotta prove everything in that hearing. They fuck me over and I'll have their asses in court—excuse me, Janine— and they know it."

"Praise Jesus!" Juantar said.

Willis said, "Who in the hell do they think they are, trying to keep something like that secret from the public? The murderer knows who he killed—no sense keeping it from him. What were they thinking? Did they think they could keep it a secret forever? Protecting their butts was all they were doing, stupidly trying to buy time. Isn't that right, Chauvin?" Willis was beginning to respect Juantar because Juantar was willingly sharing in the danger below.

"Oh my, I should say so," Juantar said. He looked pious and pretended to pray. "Please deliver us all some good porking, Lord," he said. "Believe me, we need it badly."

"Amen," Janine said. Her hand was disconcerting on my thigh.

It was difficult for me to keep my hands off

her when we felt our way through the darkness of the underground sidewalks. I let my hand stray onto her rump as we stepped into the darkness of the sidewalk, but moved it quickly as though it had been an accident.

Janine grabbed my hand and put it back on her rump. "Oh, don't be so damn civilized," she said. What she wanted was a little human warmth before she stepped off into the labyrinth to face a psycho. I was in the market for some company, too, and we held one another for a moment. Finally she said, "After you, big guy."

"Yes, ma'am. We'll finish this later then? The fooling-around part."

"Yes, yes, later, Mr. Denson."

Janine Hallen was an extraordinary woman. One side of her was reserved and properly distant. She was conservative in her dress. She was a bit shy, in fact. Her other side was playful and affectionate; she wanted to burrow right in there. She wanted to live. It was as though she had the ability to put her inhibitions on a shelf if she pleased. It was hard to keep my mind off her. I started slowly down the sidewalk with Janine close behind, her hand on my collar as was our custom on our patrols. Three or four people laughing and walking rapidly passed overhead on the street-level sidewalk. We could hear them talk because there was a small hole in the sidewalk with a dim shaft of light coming down from a streetlamp above.

One man said, "Man, the Sonics play defense? Play D? What are you talking about? If you leave Jimmy Paxson out on that wing by himself he's gonna pop 'em in all night long. The Sonics win a few, then say shee-it, no reason to bother with D. Just how long does it take them to learn is what I want to know. Makes a lot of sense. Win on the road and come back here and lose to the Blazers. God, Portland!" His exclamation was in disgust, as though there was no more humiliating spectacle on the planet than watching the Sonics lose to the Trail Blazers at home.

It wasn't more than two or three minutes after the basketball people passed that I heard a faint buzzing. A saw! Juantar had been right.

Janine squeezed the back of my neck to let me know she heard it, too. The sawing stopped and she released her grip. The sawing started and she tightened it.

The sawing stopped. I punched the light on my watch. Twelve-forty.

We waited, not breathing.

At last, Janine said, "Juantar was on this side when he heard it."

"Was there anything about those plans to go across the streets that would account for a tunnel in this side?" I whispered.

"This stretch along here is the shortest distance to Pioneer Place. The street up there is narrow."

"Then they could have started their project along here?"

"Could have," she said. "Makes sense. It'd be cheapest and easiest from here."

"And it somehow got covered up, got hidden over the years?"

"That's possible, too. Wouldn't take much to disguise a hole in the wall."

"Only to get uncovered recently. How?" I asked.

Janine said, "A few years ago they had to reinforce the sidewalks along here. Maybe then."

I said, "A workman, possibly. A bricklayer."

"Prib Ostrow, you're thinking."

I didn't say anything. I checked my wristwatch. We still had a few yards to go for a twenty-minute break. We eased on down the sidewalk and stopped at the appointed spot. We held onto one another. We listened to footsteps above. There was nothing below except for the musty smell, the silence, and the occasional stirring of a rat. The city had the underground covered with cans of poisons, but still the rodents kept coming.

It was about time to move on when I was aware of a presence. "Somebody's down here," I whispered.

Janine nodded her head yes against my shoulder.

"I feel him," I said.

She nodded again. "Me, too."

"Better get it ready."

She knew what I meant. She sat up slowly and drew the .38 from her shoulder holster.

A figure burst from an alcove not two yards

away. Pushed me hard. Pushed Janine. From the sidewalk I turned on my flashlight and aimed it down the sidewalk. The weak beam wasn't good for much.

I heard Janine cock the revolver.

There he was.

"No!" I shouted.

She didn't shoot.

He was gone. We had just glimpsed him turn the corner.

"What if it was Willie?" she said. "I couldn't shoot."

"It could have been." The figure had been wearing a red top of some kind.

Janine said, "He wasn't large enough for Prib Ostrow."

"Could have been Willie, could have been Rodney."

"Could have been Jensen or Egan too. Mike Stark."

It could have been any one of those men or a complete stranger.

We stayed below after the Doie closed. We couldn't risk going to an all-night café for coffee for fear of being monitored by Toba. At three in the morning we heard the howling again. This time the animal yipped and yelped before his howling. His howling seemed unusually lonesome and mournful; it drifted down the musty tunnels and into the empty rooms, an eerie, ghostly presence.

29 IN THE BEGINNING

The skies over Seattle were ashen and somber. Janine Hallen and I had seen it coming and had bundled ourselves in layers of sweaters, but the cold still slapped us in the face when we stepped out of the warmth of my Fiat. We joined the other people who were going to Pioneer Place Park to hear Coyote stories. The clouds thinned to a dull gray then gathered again, turning dark, charcoal and worse. They moved heavily, bloated with rain. To the west—above the Puget Sound, where freighters lay like ghosts of Sargasso—the clouds rolled toward us. They billowed. They were angry. They came low and hard, bulls, gods upset. There would be rain, but that was not unusual; it was October, and on the shores of the North Pacific coast it rained from the tenth month through the fifth, weather much beloved by ducks and fungi.

People gathered in spite of the cloudy weather. The city had planted shrubs in the interior to keep bums from sleeping there and hoped that would discourage the gathering. The organizers, assured by the police that it was safe at the tiny park despite the manhunt for the butcher murderer, went ahead with their plans. The folks standing among the shrubs wanted to hear Indian storytellers. They were there to support Native Americans in spite of the butcher. They thought they were being slightly heroic in doing that and were thrilled. Later—after discussions of herpes, AIDS, and ex-spouses had flagged—there would be spooky stories to tell while they sipped fruity white wine in front of a nice fire.

They stood on sodden wet grass, moisture oozing over the soles of their shoes. Those standing among the wet shrubs had wet pantlegs. They shifted from side to side to keep their feet warm. In keeping with their status, the intellectuals among them smoked pipes; some wore spectacles that steamed over. They breathed in lazy, frosty streams and talked in quick, frosty puffs. They had old umbrellas at the ready. They were not people who lived in A-frame houses. They lived in old cottages and bungalows that they had restored themselves. They bought their sweaters from Fred Meyer's or K-Mart and drove old Saabs and Peugeots that were hard to start in the morning. They were teachers, librarians, people who lingered over the newspaper in the morning.

They wore layers of wool to keep body heat in. They wore tans and browns, drabs, the colors of winter, although the city was treed by conifers that were always green. They wore woolen caps pulled down over their ears. They wore mittens and warm gloves that had been Christmas presents the year before. They stood with their backs to the wind that preceded the inevitable rain. Their comfortable old Hush Puppies were soaked. The wind pushed their clothes tight against their bodies and slapped the hoods of their rain slickers. They clutched mimeographed leaflets, incorrectly punctuated, that explained the storytelling function of an Indian shaman, or medicine man.

One of the functions of the shaman, the pamphlet said, was to explain the past. The natives of the Americas believed, as their Asian ancestors believed before them, that life travels in circles. That what once was, will be again. That's why the old stories were important; in telling the stories, the shaman told how things were in the beginning. First, there was the Great Spirit. The Great Spirit made the Animal People who came before man. One of these Animal People was Coyote, who was a prankster, and who could change himself into a human if necessary to tell stories of how the world began and how things of value were preserved. These stories varied from tribe to tribe, but that didn't make any difference. A Clallam had his world. A Yakima had another.

The proceedings began with a middle-aged Indian man who wore an old cowboy hat with a dirty sweatband. He wore a Levi's jacket that was open in front. He wore a western-style shirt with turquoise trim and mother-of-pearl snaps. He had a hard little belly. The huge buckle of his belt had the Budweiser beer trademark on the front. His black hair was woven into a thick braid at the back of his head. He stood on the front edge of the wooden platform that had been erected on the park side of the totem pole. He snapped a microphone around his neck. "Testin', testin', one, two," he said. "Testin', testin'."

The pot-bellied Indian put his hand over the microphone and said something to a woman standing at the base of the platform. He faced the park again. We in the park looked up at him, waiting. The noises of the flu and colds made a little symphony: someone coughed; the cough was echoed on the opposite of the park; two or three noses were blown; there was a flurry of snuffling. "Good mornin' ladies and gentlemen," he said. "It's nice to see you all out here in spite of the Seattle sunshine. My name is Leon Tallfir. I'm a Puyallup. It's supposed to be my job to explain the stuff on this here piece of paper written by my daughter-in-law, which even she admits doesn't make much sense." He laughed and looked at the woman at the base of the platform, who laughed, too, and looked a little embarrassed. Everyone applauded. Thereupon, Leon set about to explain the stilted and confused description of myths and medicine men on the mimeographed sheet. Between the paper and Leon everybody got the gist of what shamans were all about.

Tallfir's voice was tinny and distant on the

cheap microphone. He held the brim of his hat as he talked. He said, "If you're the kind of person who watches TV all the time, you might not get much out of these stories. TV's a great big tit, as I'm sure Coyote himself would say. Folks suckle up to the darn thing but don't get much out of it. These stories are magic like you can sometimes find in a good book, only we didn't have books so the stories had to be memorized and still are. They've been told and retold because they are truth, you betcha. This is what happened."

Tallfir started to unsnap the microphone from his neck, but he had one more thing to say. He gestured toward the group of Indian men, including Willie Prettybird, who waited their turn at one end of the platform. "These men are from various tribes here in the Pacific Northwest. They'll tell you who they are. One thing I suspect, though, is that Coyote himself is probably one of them. I can't imagine Coyote knowing we were going to tell stories about him—which he knows we're doin', believe me— without gettin' in on the proceedin's. There was an article in the paper tellin' about today's storytellin' in which one of the brothers of the park here let it out that Coyote wears a red bandana. In view of that, our storytellers today all agreed to wear red bandanas so the real Coyote might blend in and not be an object of curiosity on the eleven o'clock news. You'll have to decide for yourself who the real Coyote

is." Tallfir laughed at that, and so did everybody else.

Sure enough, that was true. No matter if he
was dressed in buckskins or blue jeans, each
man wore a red bandana around his neck. In
view of the politics of their white supporters,
the absence of a female medicine man must
have been of some concern; Indian shamans
were traditionally as male as McSorley's Bar in
New York before women's lib. Tallfir didn't
want to get into an argument. He chose to say
nothing. No jokes. Nothing. The mimeographed
paper said the ten storytellers represented such
diverse tribes as the Kittitas, the Klickitat, the
Clallam and the Cowlitz, the Yakimas, the
Wahkiakum, the Snohomish, Skokomish, and
the Swimomish. The ancestors of these gentlemen were around long before Eric the Red set
sail to export VD to the Americas.

The first modern-day medicine man to speak
was a Clallam named James Whitefish, who
was dressed in a buckskin getup that was
really something. There were leather fringes
down the backs of the sleeves and the legs.
Whitefish wore a feathered headdress and moc-
casins that looked soaked and cold. He carried
a tambourine-like instrument made of rawhide,
which he whacked rhythmically with a stick.
He went, *"Neah huh huh!"* Whack! Whack!
Whack! *"Neah huh huh!"* Whack! Whack!
Whack! He did that for three or four minutes,
working himself into a trance, before he began
telling a convoluted Coyote story that appar-

ently contained some kind of moral about men who beat their wives and wives who were indifferent to sex. Both kinds of behavior were to be avoided.

I was cold and dug my hands deeper in my coat pockets. I had the urge to warm them up with my crotch but remained civilized out of respect to Janine. I got lost in Whitefish's story and started watching the crowd.

I found something there that was just shy of stunning. Not one, but both of the Prettybirds' adversaries—Foxx Jensen and Doug Egan—were among those watching. One with a dog and a motive, the other with a love of saws and a motive. They were on opposite sides of the park from one another. Mike Stark was in the crowd, too, looking merry as usual. "Hey," I said to Janine, "did you see . . ."

"Egan and Jensen. Yes. Here to see if these people are going to talk about their lawsuits. And Mike Stark. Look over there to our left." She nodded her head in the direction of Rodney Prettybird and his friend Prib, standing on either side of Melinda Prettybird who had ventured out of seclusion to hear her older brother tell his Coyote story.

George was at Jensen's side, seemingly oblivious to the rain. I whistled in the dog's direction. "Hey, George! Remember me?" George did indeed, and came a-running for a nuzzle behind his ears.

Foxx Jensen beamed. "Old George likes to have his ears rubbed," he called. "Miserable weather, ain't it, Mr. Denson? Dogs like it, though."

I lowered my voice so Jensen couldn't hear me. "George, was that you in the underground the last couple of nights? Down there howling like that. Was it, boy? Tell old John the truth."

George looked up at me with trusting brown eyes. His tongue slopped out over his teeth from the excitement of being in a crowd of people who competed for a chance to nuzzle his ears.

I looked at Willie waiting his turn and couldn't take my eyes off him. Willie was dressed in blue jeans, a red ski-jacket, and an Irish walking hat as might be worn by Rex Harrison or Laurence Olivier. He fiddled with his red bandana and stared at his cowboy boots. He held a small paper bag. He looked morose, depressed. Willie was ordinarily optimistic, ebullient. Not now. I had never seen him look so sad. He was not the kind of person to suffer stage fright. Not Willie. This was something far worse.

Willie Prettybird was fourth on the list of storytellers. The rain suddenly swept across the park as Willie ascended the wooden stairs. Umbrellas popped as he appeared on the platform, his ski-jacket a shocking red. He stared out at us, clutching his paper bag, while Tallfir fastened the microphone around his neck. He began directly: "My name is Willie Prettybird. I'm a Cowlitz. This story was told to me by my grandfather. I don't think it was originally

Cowlitz because it begins in the headwaters of the Yakima. That doesn't matter because it's a good story. It could be Cowlitz, I'd be pleased if it was. This story is how our part of the world came to be made."

30 COYOTE

Splatters of rain leaped and hopped on the unpainted plywood at Willie Prettybird's feet. He looked up at the clouds and grinned. He pulled the hood of his scarlet ski-jacket up over his head. He looked down at us and adjusted the microphone that lay on the red bandana at his throat. He began:

"Once a long time ago a beaver monster named Wishpoosh lived in Cle Elum Lake, high up in the Cascades above Yakima, and was keeping the fish from the Animal People. He wouldn't go dibs, which was the fair thing to do, then as now. The Animal People asked the Great Spirit for help, and the Great Spirit sent Coyote, who was living out there in the Horse Heaven Hills south of where Hanford is now." Willie waved in the direction of Mt. Rainier, which was invisible behind the clouds. Hanford, as we all knew, was the atomic plant that, along with reactors at Oak Ridge, Tennessee, had furnished fuel for the Manhattan Project in World War II.

"So Coyote went there. He ran across hot

sand where the wind blows all day. He trav-
eled up the Yakima Valley and up to the valley
that led to the lake. He ran up hot arroyos,
running at the base of rim rock in the late
afternoon. He ran across plateaus of cactus and
sagebrush. He went up, up, through foothills.
He ran past scrub juniper and jack pine. When
he got to Lake Cle Elum he found the beaver
monster. Wishpoosh was a hateful bastard.
Coyote said Wishpoosh had to share the fish
with the Animal People, but Wishpoosh said
no. He said the fish were his. He said if Coyote
wanted to take some anyway, he was welcome
to try." Here Willie Prettybird stopped. He
considered his story. He looked at Jensen and
Egan in the crowd below him.

Mike Stark held up a clenched fist. "Yeah,
Willie!"

Willie Prettybird said, "Hell, Coyote didn't
have any choice but to take him on. The
Animal People had to have fish in order to live.
The Animal People didn't want all the fish,
mind you." The rain began coming harder.
Willie cleared his throat. Nothing would stop
him from finishing his story. "Wishpoosh bared
his teeth. Coyote sighed. They had at it.
Wishpoosh and Coyote fought and struggled,
and as they battled, the waters of Cle Elum
Lake followed and made the Yakima River. It
was a terrible battle. Coyote did his best, but
the beaver monster was stronger. Coyote needed
help and asked the advice of a woman in red
who was a mushroom and lived in his stomach."

Willie Prettybird looked toward his lawyer and grinned. Janine nodded her head in acknowledgment and squeezed my arm. Willie reached into his paper bag and pulled out a snow-white mushroom with a shocking, white-specked scarlet cap. A person didn't have to be a mycologist to know Willie shouldn't be carrying that mushroom around. It had the look of evil, the forbidden. I knew from my earlier talk with Willie that it was a Fly Agaric. Even the white specks on the scarlet cap were startling, a warning to all but the biggest fool of fools. When *Amanita muscaria* is pictured in a mushroom book, the caption begins: POISONOUS. Willie squatted at the edge of the platform and held the mushroom out so that those up close could see it clearly.

"None of you should ever eat one of these," he said.

"Amen, brother!" shouted Juantar, who had walked across the street from the Doie to listen to the stories.

Willie said, "This is poison."

"You give Willie legal advice. Are you Willie's woman in red?" I whispered to Janine.

"I've got little red hearts on my underwear. Does that count?"

"You do?"

"You can check them out later on if you want."

After a minute Willie Prettybird stood up, saying nothing, and casually began eating the mushroom. The sight of him calmly biting into that taboo mushroom stunned even those who only suspected it might be dangerous. We could not take our eyes off him. It was as if we were watching Eve bite the fatal apple. Willie Prettybird was going to tell us a truth about ourselves.

Having finished the Fly Agaric, Willie stared at the tips of his cowboy boots. He was waiting, we knew, for the advice of the woman in red who was a mushroom and lived in his stomach. We listened in silence as he concentrated on the woman's advice. It would be a few minutes before she spoke. The wind abated momentarily and the rain changed into a wet mist. We waited with him, oblivious of cold feet and soaked trousers.

We all knew Willie wouldn't continue the story until he was satisfied that it was time. "Kinda makes me queasy in the stomach," he said, and we all laughed nervously.

"Take your time, Willie," someone said. I looked and saw it was Mike Stark. Stark held up a clenched fist in support of the red-clad figure on the stage.

"Is Willie going to be okay?" Janine whispered.

"He knows what he's doing," I said.

"You know, making a river took a lot out of Coyote. But he was a fighter. So was Wishpoosh. Neither one of them would give up. The earth rumbled and erupted as they fought. They fought so hard they made big holes in the mountains around them. Their fury emptied

the clouds, which filled up the holes and made
lakes. You've never seen rain like that. It took
Coyote and Wishpoosh three weeks to battle
through a ridge and make Union Gap. It took
them eight days of bitter fighting to create the
bend where the Big River bends near Wallula
and heads west."

The Big River Willie was talking about was
the Columbia. The bend where the Columbia
turns west from south wasn't too far from
Cayuse, Oregon, where I grew up listening to
the howling of coyotes in the Horse Heavens.
Both Foxx Jensen and Doug Egan were listening intently to every word of the story.

"Yes, Willie," someone said.

"The hateful Wishpoosh dragged Coyote on
and on. The waters of the lakes followed behind. The monster tore through the high mountains and made the gorge where the Big River
now flows. Coyote and Wishpoosh plunged
through a ridge and made a bridge across the
river. They pulled rocks from the shores and
made waterfalls. Of course, the bridge fell in
later." Willie was talking about the Bridge of
the Gods, a land bridge said to have once
spanned the Columbia, and about Multnomah
Falls, which plunges 620 feet off a cliff in the
fabulous gorge.

"Well, after Coyote and Wishpoosh battled
their way through the high mountains, they
came to the mouth of the Columbia down past
Astoria where the big river flows into the
ocean. Coyote was worn out. He was so tired

he almost drowned in the waves. Muskrat laughed at him. Wishpoosh continued to eat. He grabbed whales and ate them. He ate seals. He tried to get all the salmon. He threatened to kill everything in sight. He wanted everything: More! More! More! He ate, and he ate, and he ate! He took, and took, and took!" Willie's voice rose higher, higher, higher, until he was nearly screaming. He glared at Jensen. Glared at Egan. He was in a fury. His feral eyes bore in on those assembled below him.

"Yes, Willie!" Stark shouted.

Rodney Prettybird shouted above the crowd, "You tell 'em, brother Willie. You tell 'em, man. Tell the mothers. Tell the mothers where to go."

Willie was possessed, freaked out; he paced back and forth, eyes blazing. "Coyote knew he needed help. So he asked the woman in red who was the mushroom in his stomach what he should do." Willie looked at Janine again. "She told him to make himself into a branch of a fir tree and let himself be swallowed by Wishpoosh. She told him to take a stone knife with him. Coyote floated out to the beaver monster and Wishpoosh swallowed him.

"Once he was inside Wishpoosh's stomach, he changed back into his animal form again and began to hack at the heart of the monster. He hacked and chopped and slashed until Wishpoosh was dead. Then Coyote made himself small and climbed out of Wishpoosh's throat. Muskrat, who had laughed at Coyote earlier, helped him drag Wishpoosh's body up on the beach near the mouth of the Big River. Everybody helped. With his sharp knife, Coyote cut up the big body of Wishpoosh. 'Now then,' Coyote said. 'From your body, Wishpoosh, I will make a new race of people. They will live near the shores of Big River and along the streams that flow into it.' From the lower part of Wishpoosh, Coyote made the people who were to live along the coast. 'You shall be the Chinook Indians,' he said to some of them. 'You shall live near the mouth of the Big River and shall be traders. You shall live along the coast,' he told others. 'You will live in villages facing the ocean and shall get your food by spearing salmon and digging clams. You shall always be short and fat and have weak legs.'

"From the legs he made the Klickitats. 'You shall be fast and smart, famous runners and great horsemen.' From the arms he made the Cayuse: 'You shall be powerful with bow and arrows.' He made the Yakimas: 'You shall be helpers and protectors of all the poor people.' He made the Nez Perce: 'You shall live in the valleys of the Kookooskia and Wallowa rivers. You shall be great in council and speechmaking. You shall be skillful horsemen and brave warriors.'" Willie once again moved to the edge of the platform and squatted so he could be close to his listeners. We all moved closer so we could see the anguish in his dark brown eyes.

"From here . . ." Willie put his hand over his

heart ". . . he made the Cowlitz: 'You shall be fishermen and shall live off the salmon that come to your river.' Then . . ." Willie stopped. He stood and made huge scooping motions with the upturned palms of his hands. He suddenly began shouting:

"Coyote gathered up Wishpoosh's shit and hurled it far to the east, over the big mountains!" He shouted louder, louder. " 'You shall be people of blood and violence!' " His face was hard. He was furious, enraged at the beaver monster. He gestured to the east with scorn and disdain. "Take your shit! Take your greed! Take it!"

Willie Prettybird was finished with his story. There was a silence followed by an eerie, prolonged applause. Those who had listened to Willie were gripped with emotion. The shared moment was so powerful it raised goosebumps on the back of my neck. Janine Hallen wiped moisture from her eyes with the back of her hand.

Willie gave the microphone to Leon Tallfir and took his place by the side of the platform while the others told their stories. It was impossible for me to pay much attention to the storytellers who followed. Neither Janine nor I could take our eyes off Willie Prettybird.

When the storytelling and the fund-raising speeches were finished, we made our way to Willie, who was the center of attention of a small group of men and women who wanted to be at once Bohemian and fashionable. Mike

Stark stood on the fringes grinning his jolly grin.

Willie had returned to his affable self. He slipped an arm around his sister Melinda's waist and gave her a hug. Rodney and Prib were there, too, looking distracted, high on something. Willie seemed happy to see Janine and me. "How'd I do?" he asked cheerfully. "Did you understand what I was saying?"

"Wasn't he wonderful?" Melinda said.

"Sensational," I said. "Better than a yodeler on *The Gong Show*."

Willie was pleased. "Oh, good. Good. Let's go over to the Doie and drink a couple beers, what do you say? Or how about some of Juantar's hot wine? Do us good. This is Halloween, remember. We promised Juantar. We can throw a few darts. Play some low box or Killer. Get ready to be humiliated, Assholete. I'm going to have you whimpering." Chief Dumbshit demonstrated his dart-throwing ability with two make-believe throws at a pretend board. He had good form, a smooth stroke. His elbow was under his hand. On his second throw he said, "You're going to have to get off the streets, sis. Mike Stark was out there in the crowd."

"Oh, Willie," she said.

"I said go!" Willie looked hard at his sister. "Willie!"

"You're just going to have to stay out of sight until we get this thing resolved. Right, Rodney?"

"That's what I told her when she said she wanted to come down here," Rodney said. With that and with Prib Ostrow right behind them, Rodney started guiding his sister by the arm.

Melinda let herself be led, but she didn't want to go. "Well, would you please do something, Willie. I'm getting tired of watching soap operas all day."

When she was gone, I said, "Willie, did I ever tell you I grew up on a farm outside of Cayuse, Oregon? When I was a kid I used to listen to coyotes across the Columbia howling in the Horse Heavens."

Willie looked surprised. "Why, no. You didn't tell me. Maybe you know a little about Coyote then."

31 WE'RE ON OUR WAY, DENSON

The weather, having drenched the Indian story-telling in the afternoon, backed off, giving the kids a break that Halloween night. The clouds were merely threatening, a ten percent chance of rain the weatherman said. A person has a chance with ten percent, but if the weatherman in Seattle says there is a twenty percent chance of rain, take your umbrella. If he says ninety percent, make sure your outboard has gas and good sparkplugs.

Willie had become something of a celebrity in the Doie because of his performance across the street, so it was easy for Janine and me to duck out to go take a nap. After a couple of hours' rest we drove back to the Doie to participate in Frighten Your Neighbor Night before we went underground. Kids were all over the place, out in force. Anticipating a haul, they carried the biggest bags they could find. There were little tykes hardly able to walk and five- and six-year-olds freaked out with excitement. We saw toddlers who were Tinkerbells, four-year-olds who were Long John

Silvers. We saw ghosts, vampires, and kids in cardboard boxes made up to look like robots. A bunny rabbit with a fluff of cotton safety-pinned to her rear skipped merrily along with a kid in a rubber gorilla mask. Grinning mothers watched the carnival from the sidewalks, on the alert for screwballs. The only people out of sorts were the teenagers, who lurked on the street corners, plagued by zits and now judged too old for trick-or-treating.

I wore my black woolen pullover cap and rubbed some charcoal under my eyes. I wore my navy blue turtleneck sweater, blue jeans, and running shoes. I had a Spanish bota of screw-top red and a paper bag of raw vegetables so Janine and I could have a little snack if we wanted.

Janine wore a solid black outfit with a beret and huge fake pearls. She went heavy on the makeup and smoked her cigarette through an ivory holder. She said, "And you are a cat burglar, I take it."

"I was inspired by that movie with Cary Grant and Grace Kelly. And you are?"

"A woman who wants to blend in with the darkness of the Seattle underground. An artist or writer, the way I see it." Janine paused. "I couldn't go to sleep for thinking about Willie's performance."

I geared down for a stop sign. "It was a show-stopper, I'll say that. By the way, you can call me Cary if you want and look swoony-eyed like Grace Kelly."

For weeks the regulars at the Doie had been urged by Juantar Chauvin to come in full, rip-roaring drag—costumes all the way. Juantar had goaded them, challenged them. He said, dammit, this was the doie, not the lookie or the feelie. Freak your neighbor, he said. Freak 'em out. Thus encouraged, they responded with enthusiasm. There couldn't have been a more bizarre place in the city that night. In addition to the door prizes, everyone in costume got drinks at half price. I don't think a customer in the place was paying full price. Ordinarily shy women had transformed themselves from spectators into sultry French hookers, belly dancers, and exotic concubines. The men wore all manner of rubber masks. There was a man who looked like Jabba the Hut from *Return of the Jedi*, corpulent body and all. I saw Lucifer strolling through the crowd, casting spells and passing out cards that said "Cancer," "Bankruptcy," or "One hour with Howard Cosell." Hitler was there, chatting amiably with Jimmy Carter and an almost naked woman wrapped in huge plastic snakes. Richard Nixon was kissing Little Bo-Peep.

As Janine and I passed by, the rubber-faced Nixon said, "Really, baby, I don't have herpes. Don't you believe me?"

Even Richard Willis had managed to dig up a frilly shirt and western string tie so he wouldn't look out of place walking into the Doie. "Well?" he said. He adjusted the string tie.

I appraised his outfit. "Doc Holliday or Buck Bohannon, I'll have to think about it."

"I wonder where that damn Chauvin is?"

"We're not going under until eleven, Richard. He'll be here. He probably wants to have some fun with his costume first."

We tried for an hour to figure out which one of the figures was Juantar but gave it up. At five to eleven, and with Willis beginning to get impatient, it was decided that Janine and I would go ahead. Willis would wait for Juantar. We walked to the underground entrance on the north side of James Street, where both we and Juantar had heard the buzzing. Janine watched while I went through the lock with a state-of-the-art pick provided by Willis.

The howling began minutes after we had stopped at the first station designated by the computer. We had to coerce Willis to give the computer the times and locations of the sound we thought might have been a saw; the machine considered the data and altered our routine.

The coyote seemed especially agitated that night. He didn't howl at all at first. He fell instead into fits and spells of excited barking. Janine and I had learned from previous nights there was no sense in chasing him. He was here. He was there. We could never find him. And after the coyote stories earlier in the day, my imagination raced like a stuck blender. I started to chew on a carrot, but the crunching sound seemed outrageous under the circumstances. There was no way to hide it. I was sure the coyote could hear it. I finally removed the carrot from my mouth with my fingers. Janine knew what I was doing and could barely keep from laughing. Both of us were scared silly.

Then we both heard a buzzing. An electric saw.

"Got your weapon ready?"

Janine took her .38 from her shoulder holster.

The buzzing continued. Then stopped.

It started again.

I should have carried a weapon like everyone else. I slipped my hand into my pocket and furiously rubbed my Doie coin with my thumb. The buzzing continued.

I gave Richard Willis two beeps on the walkie-talkie—the signal for buzzing heard.

Willis gave me three beeps in return: received and understood. He and Juantar would head for the James Street underground. Willis would enter from the north, around the corner. Juantar would take the longer way and enter from the east.

I heard voices.

Janine gripped my thigh. She'd heard them, too.

I gave Richard Willis four clear beeps: voices heard, please hurry.

Willis gave me a staccato of beeps: he and Juantar were doing their best.

More buzzing.

I rubbed my Doie coin.

More voices.

I rubbed it faster, faster. Come on, Dickie! I thought.

The voices were louder.

Whatever it was that sounded like a coyote heard it, too. The sorrowful lament began. It was startlingly close to Janine and me. It got louder, louder, higher and more impassioned. The howling filled up the underground sidewalk and was all around us. It was impossible to tell which direction it was coming from, but I thought from the east, maybe—Juantar's assignment.

To hell with the beeping routine. "For Christ's sake, get your asses over here," I whispered harshly into the walkie-talkie.

My walkie-talkie clicked and I could hear a man running, breathing hard. "We're on our way, Denson, keep your pecker up."

What happened next came all in a rush.

32 EARLY IN THE MORNING

A door opened from the streetside wall. This wall had appeared solid to us and was represented by unbroken lines on the maps Janine had uncovered in her research. The open door flooded the underground sidewalk with light. Janine and I both covered our eyes. We'd become adjusted to the darkness and were momentarily blinded, helpless. We looked away from the light, not moving. The voices became clear. Men's voices. A woman said something. The voices were loud, crazed. A man spoke. He was right beside us. It was he who had opened the door. We heard a man vomiting inside.

"Oh, Jesus, Jesus, we shouldn't'a done that," a man said.

Whoever had opened the door didn't answer. He was vomiting as well. "Halloween! Shit," he said, and puked again.

The man farther inside was in terrible shape. He retched and retched and retched. "Aw God, God, we shouldn't'a done that."

The woman groaned pitiably. "Ohhhhh!" she wailed. "Ooooo. Aaaaa." We heard her vomit.

All that and the furious howling seemed right on top of us, a wavering, piercing, angry howl.

When my eyes were adjusted to the light, I stood and edged around the open door. Rodney Prettybird, on his hands and knees, was nearest the entrance. Farther down the mystery tunnel was Prib Ostrow, on his back, an awful bile erupting from his mouth. Prib was lying by a rotary brick saw. On top of the brick saw was part of a frozen human torso.

To the left of the brick saw, Melinda Prettybird squatted weakly, looking up with dull, glazed eyes. The front of her blouse and the thighs of her jeans were soaked with vomit. She opened her mouth and made gagging sounds but nothing came.

Farther down the tunnel, under the shaft that apparently rose to the center of Pioneer Place Park, I counted four RV propane freezers containing what I knew must be what was left of Moby Rappaport and Kim Hartwig.

I was glad only to see that Willie Prettybird was not in the tunnel.

Rodney Prettybird looked up at me, his face twisted.

"Why?" I asked.

"You must learn to honor your word, white man," he said. Rodney didn't recognize me as his brother's friend. I was a white man, any white man.

"We gave the judge and his helper what they

deserved. Ain't that right, Prib? Cut 'em up like animals."

"Aarrgghh!" the pribliged character said. I wasn't certain whether or not he understood Rodney.

"That's not enough, Rodney."

"We did it for those guys. Those guys up there." Rodney motioned to the ceiling of the tunnel. "Have you seen them up there? Have you? Drunk. No future. You people came with your judges and took everything we had. We signed treaties. What good did it do? What good? Took our timber. Won't let us have our salmon. We got 'em, didn't we, Prib?"

Prib didn't answer. He looked glassy-eyed.

"Threw their pieces up there where my brothers gather. Prib?"

"Aagghh."

"In the shadow of the totem pole," Rodney said. He gagged and tried to vomit, but nothing came.

Melinda Prettybird had by now slumped against the wall of the tunnel. She was unable to speak. She was too weak to vomit if she wanted to. She was in a stupor, clinging to consciousness. Her mouth hung open. Her jaw was slack. Her eyes were glazed.

Janine put her pistol back in its holster. "Look," she said.

She meant two cardboard boxes of dried mushrooms. I could tell by the red tops, even when they were dried, that one box was *Amanita muscaria*, Fly Agaric—the same as Willie

Prettybird had eaten earlier in the day. The mushrooms in the second box had white stalks and dirty yellow tops.

"How many did you eat?" I asked Prib.

He continued to retch. He tried to speak but no sound would come.

I turned to go for a phone, and there stood Rodney Prettybird, reeling but on his feet, holding an enormous revolver. He wavered. He gagged. He pointed the revolver at Janine Hallen. He cocked the revolver. Rodney Prettybird grinned. "Gonna kill you," he said.

Janine, whose pistol was back in its holster, stared at him, hands at her sides, surprised, shocked, not knowing what to do.

But Rodney's trigger finger didn't get to finish the pull. Rodney's body was suddenly hurled backward by an ear-splitting roar from the underground sidewalk. Crimson loops of blood squirted from the cavity where his heart had been.

Willie Prettybird, still dressed in his scarlet ski-jacket and red bandana, stood in the doorway with a Winchester Model 94, a lever-action .30–.30 handy for a saddle scabbard. It was Willie's deer-hunting rifle. He leaned the rifle against the wall and sat down on top of one of the RV freezers. He looked at his stricken sister, looked down at his childhood friend Prib Ostrow, who writhed in agony on the floor.

"I'll go call the ambulance," Janine said.

Willie looked at Melinda, who was fading

fast, looked at the dull yellow mushrooms. "Tell 'em to bring lots of atropine."

"Will they live?" I asked. I watched Janine disappear, running, up the underground sidewalk.

"If they're lucky." Willie picked up a dried mushroom. "*Amanita pantheria.* I once told Rodney that an *Amanita pantheria* had the same poisons as *Amanita muscaria* only more of them. You shouldn't mess around with mushrooms unless you know what you're doing." Willie knelt and wiped the sweat from his sister's feverish brow. "It's suicidal to eat these things. An ambulance is on its way, sis. Hold on." He looked at the corpse of his younger brother.

"I'm sorry it turned out this way, Willie."

"It's not your fault, John. After a while I suppose it got to be too much for Rodney, all this arguing in court for what was ours in the first place. It was outrageous. I just assumed Rappaport would rule in our favor. How could he do anything else?" Willie shook his head in amazement.

"You came with a rifle. How long have you known about Rodney and Prib?"

Willie looked at me. "And Melinda. Several days now. I've been down here nights trying to find out where they were holed up. If they'd gotten themselves worked up enough to butcher people, I thought I'd better bring some protection. I don't own a pistol so I brought my thirty-thirty."

"There's been something down here howling," I said. "Did you hear the howling?"

"I heard it, too. Figured it was some kind of dog. People shouldn't keep dogs in the city. Dogs need room to roam around."

"Or maybe some kids getting worked up for Halloween."

"Sure, that could be it," he said.

Richard Willis arrived then, breathing hard. He looked at the hole in Rodney's chest, at Willie holding his sister, and at Prib wallowing in vomit.

"Janine's on her way to get an ambulance," I said.

"Jesus Christ!"

"Will two live ones for the courts do you any good at your hearing?" I felt like vomiting myself, only not from being sick in the stomach.

Willis squatted beside Rodney's corpse. He looked at Willie, who held his sister even tighter. "My name is Richard Willis. I'm a cop. You don't have to tell me anything until you've got a lawyer. Do you understand?" Willis was kindly, genuinely concerned.

Willie Prettybird nodded. "I understand," he said.

"If you do tell me anything it can be used in court against you."

"I understand. I killed him. Shot him with my thirty-thirty."

I said, "Rodney was about to waste Janine with that thing on the floor." I nudged Rodney's pistol with my foot. "It was Rodney or her."

Juantar arrived next, also breathing hard. He wore a raincoat and a fedora. He was bleeding from both ears, both nostrils, and the corners of his mouth. A long, obscene open wound curved across his forehead and down the side of his face. Plastic maggots fed on plastic pus that had gathered in the realistic plastic wound. He looked at Rodney, then at Melinda and Prib. "Praise Jesus," he said and for the first time since I'd known him, Juantar Chauvin was momentarily moved to silence. He didn't twitch or jerk. He didn't rub the balding front of his head. He didn't wave his arms. He didn't pace. He stared at the terrible scene. "Six-bit doie," he finally said. "Much too exotic for my taste."

33 EPILOGUE

With Janine Hallen's help, Willie Prettybird was released on his own recognizance and drove downstate to Mossyrock to tell his mother what had happened. Willie had had to kill Rodney. Both Melinda and Prib Ostrow had O.D.'d on poisonous mushrooms and were seriously ill. If Melinda lived, she would likely be tried for obstruction of justice for having slept with Kim Hartwig to learn of Rappaport's decision, for abetting in Rodney's assault on Hartwig and two other of her lovers, and for assisting in the murder of Rappaport and Hartwig.

It was starting to get light when Willis, Juantar, Janine, and I went to a seafood restaurant on Alaskan Way that stayed open all night.

Juantar Chauvin was hyper again, recalling the pleasures of doie, trying to get our minds and the conversation off the Prettybirds. He wanted to cheer us up. "Hey," he said, "with all that excitement, I didn't get to show y'all the rest of my costume." He stood up and unbuttoned the front of his raincoat. There was a huge, stuffed, homemade penis sewn onto the front of his blue jeans. The bizarre organ hung to Juantar's knees. He was pleased. He swung it merrily. He wiggled his hips. He looked lascivious. He waggled his eyebrows at Janine. "Trick or treat," he said.

"Put that thing away and sit down, Juantar," Janine said.

Juantar sat. "Praise the Lord," he said.

Richard Willis said the meal was on him. He said he'd figure out some way to bill it to the department, which at least owed us all a good meal for saving its collective rump. He thereupon ordered scallops. Juantar went for Dungeness crab.

Janine studied the menu. "I think I'll have number seven," she said. "Poached salmon. Expensive, but why not? The cops are paying."

She was right about one thing: salmon was damned expensive.

"And you, sir?" the waitress asked me.

"I think I'll take number four there." I waited for the waitress to mark my order on her pad. "Just for the halibut," I said.

Juantar said, "Must we keep your company, Denson? Must we?"

Willis looked disgusted. "We'll all have double whiskies. Any objections?" He looked at the rest of us.

Nobody objected.

I slumped back on the red plastic cushion of my chair. The waitress brought our whiskies. I took a sip. I was tired. I thought about Willie Prettybird, who had been forced to kill his brother. I thought about Rodney Prettybird, who had been driven mad by the legal system. I thought about Prib, who had murdered out of naive loyalty. I thought about Melinda, who had destroyed her life. I thought about Jensen's greed and Egan's greed. It was early in the morning of a lonesome October of my most immemorial year.

Before the sun came up Melinda Prettybird died in the hospital. The doctors had pumped her stomach, but it was too late. Prib Ostrow, however, lived. His large bulk was credited with being able to absorb more poison than Melinda's small frame.

Because Ostrow lived, the rest of the story soon became clear. It turned out that Prib had been an employee of the contractor hired by the city to reinforce the rusting iron beams that held up the street-level sidewalks above the underground. That was how he found the closed-off tunnel that was the aborted first leg of a plan to connect the underground city—cut into isolated islands by solid streets—and save it from extinction. The tunnel builders had dug a shaft to the center of Pioneer Place that was eventually to have been the main entrance to the underground. The shaft had long since been capped, covered, and planted in turf like the rest of Pioneer Place. This was how Rodney and Prib smuggled parts of Moby Rappaport and Kim Hartwig past the police video cameras.

Three days after that awful Halloween, Prib Ostrow, following the counsel of a court-appointed lawyer, confessed to helping Rodney butcher the judge and his law clerk. At the end of the fishing-rights testimony, he said, Janine Hallen told the Prettybirds that Judge Rappaport would have the Boldt controversy on his mind when he wrote his decision, so he would be extra careful. She said justice was slow. Sure enough, Rappaport gave himself two months to deliver his final decision. She said Rappaport needed the time to develop an airtight case to back the decision he probably made halfway through the evidence. There were studies that showed that judges made up their minds fairly early on. On top of that, she said, Judge Rappaport wouldn't even write the decision himself. He would outline his arguments to his law clerk, Kim Hartwig, a young man fresh out of Georgetown University Law School.

Ostrow said Janine told the Prettybirds to be patient. None of this was out of the ordinary. The Prettybirds should read nothing into it. They would win. Just wait, she said.

But Rodney and Melinda Prettybird didn't want to wait, Ostrow said. They were impatient to know the decision. So without telling Willie—who wouldn't have put up with that kind of thing—they connived to have Melinda take Kim Hartwig for a sail on her waterbed. Guided by stars that were Melinda Prettybird's dark brown eyes and with an erection for a tiller, Hartwig, eager at the helm, told Melinda that yes, Rappaport was going to support the Prettybirds.

Alas, Ostrow said, after they had gone to all that trouble, Rodney Prettybird didn't believe Hartwig. Rodney said Hartwig was just trying to please Melinda. Hartwig was lying. In order to get the truth, Rodney beat Hartwig nearly unconscious. In order to stop the beating, Hartwig confessed that he had lied to Melinda: Rappaport was going to support Egan and Jensen.

Ostrow said Willie found out about the beating through his little nephew, who'd heard Rodney and Prib laughing about it while they drank beer and watched a ballgame on TV. Rodney and Melinda didn't want Willie to know what they had been doing, so Rodney hit upon the idea of beating up on a couple more of Melinda's lovers. That way, they reasoned, neither the police nor Willie would care who the lovers were. Melinda could blame the beatings on Mike Stark, whose jealousy was a matter of court record.

The next problem was what to do about Judge Rappaport. If Rappaport had already made up his mind on the lawsuit, Rodney reasoned, they might as well take a chance on Rappaport's replacement, Judge Louise Awdrey. So, Prib said, they kidnapped and murdered the judge. They got high on dried Fly Agaric and used Prib's brick saw to butcher the corpse. Once they did that it was easy enough to tidy things up by murdering Kim Hartwig.

After Prib Ostrow had said all this, of course, he and his lawyer claimed the confession was made under the influence of *Amanita pantheria* and was therefore not admissible in court. Prib really didn't understand what he was saying, the lawyer said. The lawyer said it was a well-known fact that the effects of *Amanita pantheria* last for hours. Besides, the lawyer said, Prib was insane at the time of the murders—this also from eating *Amanita*. Prib couldn't remember where he was or what he was doing.

Prib Ostrow's legal dodge infuriated the public and gave the television people reason to videotape all manner of people saying how outrageous it was.

In the first week of November, an indictment was handed down on Doug Egan for bribing Hartwig to tell him the details of the pending court decision. Hartwig had inadvertently aided the people's attorneys by recording the details of the transaction in a personal journal that police discovered while they were investigating his disappearance. William "Foxx" Jensen was arrested for extortion and willful destruction of property for his assaults on Jim Davis's Sal-PacInc cannery. Officials in Olympia petitioned their colleagues in Austin for the extradition of Jensen's Texan accomplice.

It was only after all this that the nearly completed brief of Judge Moby Rappaport's decision in the matter of Prettybird et al. vs. the State of Washington was found in his study. Judge Rappaport supported the Prettybird arguments right down the line. He said there was no reason the Cowlitz should be excluded because the Chehalis refused to sign the treaty. He said Governor Stevens was obliged to treat the tribes separately, not as a single entity.

Rodney Prettybird had concluded that Kim Hartwig was lying to Melinda about Rappaport's decision. In fact, Hartwig had been telling the truth. As far as I was concerned, that was a curious mistake on Rodney's part. Melinda Prettybird had the kind of eyes and charm that would make a man swear allegiance to Lucifer if she asked.

The Prettybird case was moved to the court of Judge Louise Awdrey.

Richard Willis, accompanied by Janine Hallen as his attorney, faced the police department tribunal for his alleged insubordination earlier in the year. Before the appointed hour Janine got tough with Richard. She told him he had to be calm. He had the advantage because he had gotten to the butcher killers before the department did and had let the cops take credit. News of Toba's participation had somehow remained secret, and that was Richard Willis's ace.

The chairman of the disciplinary panel, worried about protecting the department's collective behind, let Willis off with an admonition to in the future please be more patient with dumb cops.

Willie Prettybird dropped out of sight after

he was cleared. He told me he'd be back one day and to expect him to return when I saw him walking through the door. I got in touch with Captain Mikey, Scabby, the Rodent Clone, and the Beaner. We formed the First Avenue Irregulars, a dart team out of the Doie. Rodent Clone took over the job of my unofficial coach: Keep your foot down, Assholete. Slow down. Stop rolling. Extend your arm. Start it with the triple-eighteen, believe me. Zen darts now. Zen darts. When Rodent Clone was absent, Captain Mikey took over the onerous duty.

Every Sunday we played Killer at the Doie. As far as I'm concerned, above all other games, darts in general and Fuck Your Buddy in particular most approximate the vicissitudes of life: a constant struggle against loss of concentration, bad luck, and better players. The last time I was in the Doie, Willie's brethren were still sitting under the shelter of the delicate, airy pergola across the street. They had their wine with them. They smoked cigarettes. They powwowed. They told one another old fish stories.

BESTSELLING BOOKS FROM TOR